ELYSIUM

Alexa Black

Also writing as A. M. Hawke

Supposed Crimes LLC • Matthews, North Carolina

This book is a work of fiction. Names, characters, places, and incidents are products of the author's imagination or are used fictitiously. Any resemblance to actual events or locales or persons, living or dead, is entirely coincidental.

All Rights Reserved
Copyright © 2020 Alexa Black

Published in the United States.

ISBN: 978-1-952150-10-4

www.supposedcrimes.com

This book is typeset in Goudy Old Style.

To all the people who wanted these stories to have a home. Thanks for telling me so.

Table of Contents

BONNIE AND THE BEAST

THE BEAST'S tongue darted out to lick her fangs. *A woman will be coming today.*

She perched atop an old, crumbling column, ready to leap off if need be. Her two larger eyes blinked, but the triangle of three smaller eyes above them stayed open, ever watchful.

A pretty one, so the man said. Her snout twitched and sniffed the air.

She'd had a flat, round face as a human, but now her head was pointed and sharp, her closed mouth ringed with sharp, exposed fangs. Thick fur covered her face and body, a rich dark brown that shone purple when the light hit it.

They called her a werewolf.

They had no idea.

Their mistake made sense enough. Thick fur covered the back of her head and neck, and only grew thicker further down. And where she'd once been bulky, the transformation had broadened her chest and flattened her breasts. Her chest was smooth as any female animal's now.

She'd never liked frills and fancy clothing, but after the Change she'd taken to wearing men's shirts and pants, sturdy and rough-spun, as much from necessity as anything else.

She missed wearing boots, but broad feet with claws that could grasp tight served well enough. She could perch on anything that would support her altered weight and spring off of it again with the agility of a creature half her size.

Magical curses weren't all bad, she supposed, scanning the path below. Faeries were old-fashioned sorts. Ancient creatures, who'd gone into hiding when the humans built too many machines. Machines that did too many things only magic used to do.

Nowadays, only technomancers knew how to use what remained of the old machines. The devices that made things, the tablets that stored information (whole bookshelves full, if the legends were true), and all the other wonders of the ancients.

The Beast snorted. She'd seen a technomancer once as a child. He'd shown off a little machine, a tiny, light thing he'd held aloft in one hand. She could remember the strange device even now, its surface smooth and polished black, marred only by a thin crack running across it. He'd told her that with the touch of one finger, he could make it light up and fill with symbols and words. Like a sorcerer's magical book, without the riddling it usually took to convince him to let you steal a peek.

She hadn't expected much. Even as a human child, she'd known better. But she'd still pouted when the black glass revealed nothing at all.

Oh, they probably managed to make the old machines work once in a while. But however they did it, that wasn't magic, regardless of what the technomancers called themselves.

And if they really could make the old world work again, they would have done it already.

The real magical folk came back after the fall of the machines and the people who used them. But the world didn't work the way they expected it to. Not anymore.

There were princes and princesses, castles and merchants,

and all the courtly politics they'd always meddled in. The magical folk were ready to bless the ones they favored with enchantments and curse the ones they didn't happen to like.

But whatever might have become of the "computers" and the "motors," history always left its mark. Even princesses and princes could learn from what had come before.

And sometimes that made breaking curses harder, not easier.

A flash of movement pulled her from her thoughts. She opened her secondary eyes wider, hoping to catch sight of its source.

Ah, there. She let her primary eyes take over and turned her head to see better.

A young woman emerged from between the trees, short and full-figured. She moved with slow steps, like she'd been walking for a long time, but she stared straight ahead, blinking sweat and dust out of her eyes.

She wore a long gold-yellow dress, ill-suited to traipsing through the forest. The fabric had torn, and mud and dirt smeared the hem. She'd hiked it up and held the fabric tight in her hand, but there was only so much you could salvage in the woods after the rain.

She had curly, reddish hair, tied in a practical ponytail at the back of her head. Loose strands of it clung to her forehead and neck, glued there by sweat.

All normal enough. But the part that her sweat hadn't plastered to her skin didn't look like a tired traveler's hair should. Bedraggled as the woman was, her hair caught the light. It gleamed, like she was standing under full sunlight on a bright day. Not traipsing through a forest and stained all over with its dirt.

The Beast sniffed the air again. Was that just a trick of the light, or was this woman enchanted too?

She tilted her head back to howl her curiosity, but snapped her muzzle shut. *Don't frighten her. Not more than you can help.*

The woman stopped, her hand still gripping the hem of

her unfortunate dress.

Now that she'd come closer, the Beast could see big eyes, a full mouth, and of course that maybe-magical hair, still just a little too bright for the forest shade. She had a smattering of freckles across her nose and cheeks that kept her looking too human for the Beast to be sure there was magic involved.

She had the soft look of the wealthy, her skin pale and uncalloused, but she didn't look uncomfortable with the dirt or the trees or the winding path to get here.

She blinked hazel eyes—normal ones, from what the Beast could tell—and scanned her surroundings.

Then she caught sight of the Beast.

Her eyes widened. She stammered and drew back. Her lower lip trembled.

"What are you?" she whispered.

The Beast didn't answer. There would be time enough to say "Just your average cursed princess" later.

And besides, she'd never been particularly believable as a princess. Not even before she'd changed.

The girl looked at her, still staring like she was afraid. Then she drew herself up to her full height, squared her shoulders, and bit her lip to stop its quivering.

The Beast's lips pulled back from her fangs in her best approximation of a grin. Heat stirred in the Beast's breast, hidden deep under layers of fur and transmuted flesh. *You're afraid. But you're facing me anyway.*

"Is this—?" She stopped, licked her lips, and tried again. "Is this the way to Eastvale Castle?"

"It is." The Beast bowed and crooked a clawed hand in front of herself, the picture of gallantry. She'd paid attention to a few lessons about manners way back when, at least. Even if she was just envying what the princes learned instead.

The woman hiked her skirts higher. Without another spare glance for the Beast, she began to walk, lips pressed together in determination.

"I'm the one you're here to see," the Beast pressed.

A hitch in her stride. The Beast grinned to see it. But she

still didn't turn around. "Probably, yes."

"Then it's pointless to ignore me."

"The castle is yours. So are the people in it."

The Beast snuffled. "It's not like that."

"So I'm not yours until I get there."

Well. The Beast couldn't argue with that.

"At least tell me your name."

There was power in names. Any enchantress or elf could tell you that. And she probably knew it, if that hair really was a boon from the faeries.

The woman cocked an eyebrow. "My father didn't tell you?"

"He told me enough. That he knew he wasn't welcome in Eastvale. That it belonged to me. And that you would be willing to pay whatever price I demanded from him."

The woman chewed a tantalizingly thick lip. "Then my name is Bonnie," she said after a long moment.

Really now? The Beast opened her mouth to say it. Bonnie looked at her fangs and didn't blink. Interest, or fear?

"Fine," the Beast said. "Keep your name." Everyone had secrets, even humans.

She looked down at the soiled hem of Bonnie's dress, her dirty fingers. "But let me carry you. You'd be light as air to me."

That got a reaction. Bonnie turned back, looked her over. Her gaze lingered on the Beast's broad chest and strong shoulders. The Beast licked her fangs again and tried not to purr too loudly.

"And like you said," The Beast went on, all her eyes staring back, "once you get to Eastvale, you're going to have to deal with me anyway."

Bonnie laughed, but didn't take her eyes off the Beast. "If it's all the same to you, I'd rather walk."

"Suit yourself." The Beast growled.

The Beast had been right. Bonnie was tired. She trudged up the path on halting legs, even the hand on her skirt faltering. And her breath came in short gasps, unseemly for someone rich enough to be a minor noble.

The Beast hadn't been sure exactly who her father was. But she'd known he was rich, from his bearing and his ridiculous garments. Half plastered with gold, half made of antique fabrics from the time of the ancients. Or expensive copies, carefully handcrafted by artisans who'd spent long years studying how the ancients made things and doing their best to mimic them.

He'd been wearing a small fortune, either way. Why someone like that would go wandering through the forest near Eastvale, the Beast still couldn't guess.

Not that it really mattered why. The man kept his promises, and that's what was really important.

And so did Bonnie, apparently. Both the promise to come to Eastvale, despite its Beast loping along next to her in all her half-animal glory, and the promise to fend for herself. The Beast had caught her glancing at her now and then and sighing, then turning back to the road with that same determined expression she'd seen before.

I've apparently forgotten how quickly humans get tired. The Beast chuckled, a doglike whine. *Or maybe watching this one is supposed to teach me something. I guess this lesson is resilience.*

She cast her eyes skyward. *Is that right, enchantress? Have I learned something today?*

Not that whatever lesson this was supposed to impart would be enough to break the curse.

If I even want to. The Beast looked down at her clawed hands, at the purple sheen of her palms. If they shifted back to human pink, would she even recognize them anymore?

Bonnie dragged herself up the mossy steps to the door of Eastvale Castle and hesitated, catching her breath. She studied the carvings in the wood, her gaze flicking from one to the other.

They weren't pictures of the Beast. That would be entirely too straightforward for the fae folk. But they were images of chimeras and creatures. A man with a lion's mane and a yawning mouth full of rows of shark-like teeth. A winged woman with a demon's cloven hooves and a serpent's tail. Animals with the eyes and lips and tongues of men.

The door was dark too, the wood stained a bloody crimson by the spell that had cursed the Beast and her castle.

The spell—and the passage of time, to be fair—made the outside of the castle forbidding. Moldy, overgrown, and festooned with gargoyles and grotesques in the same style as the door. The enchantress who'd cursed the Beast had even tossed in a fully human grotesque, its face twisted in a rictus of despair.

A little joke, no doubt to remind the Beast of her hubris.

Bonnie bit her lip and studied the carvings, but she only hesitated a moment. She wrapped her hands around the heavy door handle and tugged. It didn't budge.

"This one you'll have to let me get for you," the Beast snapped.

Bonnie favored her with an exhausted sigh and stepped aside.

The castle belonged to the Beast, and so did its curse. The door would have opened for her even if her transformation hadn't made her strong. She barely wrapped her claws around it and it flung wide, eager to be opened.

Bonnie whistled. "Nice place."

The Beast blinked her secondary eyes. Yes, she supposed, it was a nice place. But she was used to seeing it, and as much as she appreciated the finery, she would have been fine with a few simple rooms.

Becoming a monster hadn't made the whole princess thing much more appealing.

But to Bonnie it might well be impressive. Especially after seeing Eastvale castle only from the outside.

The magic had twisted the outside of the castle to frighten visitors away, but the inside gleamed. The same magic that made the exterior warn people away kept the inside pristine. Most of it looked like it had years ago when the enchantress had cursed the Beast.

Some things the enchantments had altered. The rugs depicted animals and creatures, just as the outside had. But here, rather than grotesques and deformed monsters warning intruders away, the animals frolicked, friendly and welcoming. Similar tapestries adorned the walls, depicting both woodland wildlife and creatures like unicorns.

The wooden furniture was the same blood-dark red as the door. But in a bright room lit by ornate chandeliers, it didn't look nearly as frightening.

Apparently even enchantresses had some small amount of pity. Once someone came inside, the magic wanted to keep them there.

"Welcome," the Beast said, with another courtly bow.

She didn't hide the growl in her voice. Bonnie didn't seem like the type who needed anything papered over. And she'd seen the Beast already.

"Thank you," said Bonnie, her voice still tired. "So now what happens?"

"I was thinking about dinner." The Beast couldn't resist licking her fangs. Obligingly, Bonnie shuddered. "But you might want to wash yourself and lie down first." She sniffed. "You reek of mud and sweat."

"That bothers monsters?" Bonnie raised an eyebrow.

"Not at all. But you're a human. Humans don't like smells and dirt."

Bonnie gave her a searching look. "And why are you being so nice to a human that you're just going to eat anyway?"

"Eat you?" The Beast sidled close enough to press against Bonnie's back and leaned in. She made a show of sniffing her neck.

Bonnie really did smell like sweat, and mud, and wet leaves. And under it all, the smell of her blood, coppery and tangy and sweet, the way only humans smelled. The Beast could feel her pulse, a siren's rhythm.

She licked her fangs, full of nervous energy. Part of her wanted to press her head into the soft skin and nuzzle it. Part of her wanted to bite, to let that blood she smelled wash over her fangs.

But she couldn't. She needed this human to be more than prey.

Bonnie trembled, but didn't pull away. She lifted her head as if daring the Beast to try.

The Beast blinked, moving her head to get her nose away from that heady smell. "You thought I wanted to eat you and still came all this way?"

Bonnie laughed, a shaky sound at first, but that became something high and clear. The Beast decided she liked it. "No, I came all this way to trick you into not eating me."

"Well then," the Beast said, sweeping a hand in front of herself.

"That—just dinner? That's all?"

"Did you think I'd make demands the moment you stepped over the threshold?"

A smile quirked the corner of Bonnie's mouth. "No." Just as quickly, it vanished. "But you might do something worse. What exactly do you do with the humans you don't kill and eat? Lock them up and starve them?"

The Beast laughed. "I'm not that kind of monster."

"You could have fooled me just now, sniffing at me like a rabid wolf."

"I'm not a wolf. And if I was rabid, I wouldn't have bothered to welcome you in."

"Not a wolf?" Bonnie pulled away, but the stare she turned on the Beast was appraising, not fearful. "Then what are you?"

Her gaze swept over the Beast's body. She stared for a moment at the Beast's legs, long and slightly bent, coiled to spring at any moment. But she looked far longer at the Beast's hips, at her broad, flat chest, at the tuft of purple-sheened fur peeking out from under her shirt.

You don't mind that I'm a monster, do you? The Beast flexed her arm muscles. The transformation had enhanced those too. And hunting her own meat helped even more.

Bonnie grinned. She reached a hand to her hair, pulled

out the band around her ponytail, and shook out her curls. The light caught them, as before, a glittering dazzle.

The Beast wondered, again, what this woman was. Why she had been so coy about her name. She'd come here to save her father from the Beast and her curse, supposedly. But someone who'd come as a sacrifice would be nervous or defiant. Trembling or angry. And this Bonnie was neither.

She knows more than she lets on. And the Beast would have to ask about it. Or wrench it out of her by faerie trick or tooth and claw.

But right now, the way she was looking at the Beast mattered more. It was good. It was very good. But—

Do you like women or men?

The Beast stared back at Bonnie and tilted her head. "What am I? Whatever some faerie enchantress decided I should be."

She licked her fangs again and clenched clawed hands. "So, what do you think?"

"I think I'd better break your curse, before you decide eating me is a good idea after all."

The Beast barked with laughter. "Then you really do think you're here to break my curse."

"Think I am? My father sent me here because you would have ripped him apart if I didn't come."

Her father, again. Just a would-be rescuer. Or so she wanted the Beast to think.

"Well." The Beast looked down at her claws. "Rules are rules, and they get ugly when the fae make them."

"The fae. Not you."

The Beast growled. "I'm not all monster. But I'm not human anymore either."

Bonnie chewed her lip, but her stare ahead was clear. "So what do I have to do to break this curse?"

"I don't think you're going to manage it. I'm not sure you'll want to."

And it's not something I could demand anyway. Monster or not.

"Try me."

The Beast's rumbling became a laughing purr. "Fall in love with me."

Dinner, it turned out, was simpler.

The Beast even bothered to make sure her dinner was cooked. She wanted it raw, raw and bleeding, with bones she could crack and flesh she could tear, and a rich raw scent that would distract her from the memory of Bonnie's pulse.

But Bonnie was a human, and humans ate their food cooked. Rare meat with pink juice pooling under it was good enough, if she had a human guest. At least it was still on the bone.

Bonnie pushed her fork into the meat and sawed at it with a knife. The Beast had done the same thing herself, more times than she could possibly remember, but somehow it all looked so strange now. Delicate and dainty little pink human fingers curling around utensils making small precise cuts in the flesh of prey, like that was natural. Like eating tiny strips of it one at a time made any sense at all.

She blinked her secondary eyes in Bonnie's direction and picked up her own fork and knife. Her claws got in her own way, curling around each other and making her growl in exasperation.

Bonnie speared a piece of fruit with her fork and laughed. "Werewolf or not, go ahead and do whatever it is you want to do."

Half apologetic, the Beast picked up a bundle of grapes, opened her mouth, and tossed it in. She bit down, and the sweet flavor flooded her mouth in a burst of juice. She rarely ate fruit anymore, not when she could fill her stomach perfectly well by hunting anyway. But right now, she felt glad the sorceress had left her able to enjoy it.

Bonnie was still looking at her, one eyebrow raised. Her eyes were open, unblinking. Teasing? The Beast shivered, thinking of it. A small little human, daring her?

She made a half-hearted attempt at chewing the grapes with teeth no longer suited to the task, and then swallowed the whole bundle down. One burst of flavor was good, a bright honeyed shock to the system, but bothering to chew the stuff was something else entirely.

She lowered her muzzle to the table and tore into the meat with tooth and claw, let the pink juice smear her lips and wet her fur. It felt good, even if it wasn't enough.

And cooked food was better spiced anyway. She purred with the pleasure of it, a meal half from her remembered human life and half from her wild one.

She stretched her tongue out to lick the juice from her claws, looking at Bonnie out of her secondary eyes. What did Bonnie think of her, eating like the predator she was?

Bonnie looked back at her, not blinking. Her teeth pressed against her lower lip. They made it look even more thick and full than before, and another pulse of heat curled through the Beast's flesh. Biting that would be even more delicious than this food.

But did it mean Bonnie was nervous, or intrigued? The Beast closed all of her eyes and purred, unsure which of those she would like better.

When she opened them again, Bonnie was still looking at her, though it was impossible to tell whether that gaze was fixed on her claws, or her muzzle, or even on the mess she'd made of her plate.

But she could swear she'd noticed Bonnie shiver.

She cracked a bone in half with her hands, brought it to her mouth, and sucked out the marrow, savoring the fatty, buttery taste.

"You really are..." Bonnie whispered. She stared down at the splintered piece of bone in what the Beast hoped was horrified fascination.

The Beast let her gape a moment. Then she lifted the piece of bone to her mouth again and sucked and licked at it, making as much noise as she could manage. If Bonnie wanted a monster, the Beast might as well give her one.

She chuckled for good measure, low in her throat. "I really am. Whatever it means to you."

Bonnie looked down at the Beast's plate, at the other half of the bone still lying there.

Then she flashed the Beast a grin. "You didn't call me here just to feed me dinner."

The Beast chuckled. "No."

"Then let's go find a place to talk."

The Beast dropped the piece of bone she'd been chewing on. It hit the plate with a clatter. Servants or magic or both would attend to it, and she was trying to be dramatic.

She bowed again to Bonnie and led her away, grinning.

She didn't take Bonnie to the bedroom. Not yet.

Bonnie understood. That much was clear. And was willing to make herself a sacrificial lamb, too.

Out of curiosity or desire or both, which probably wasn't what the fae would want. And the magic would know it.

On the surface, it fit perfectly. Exactly what the magic would be looking for. A beautiful innocent's great love for her father, transmuted into love for a prideful noble turned monster.

But falling in love didn't work like that. It probably never had. Not even in the days before the machines.

So Bonnie was lounging on a couch, still in the ragged dress she'd worn coming in. Mud still stained it, and somewhere in the mists of years-old memories the Beast could hear her mother's voice, scolding her for getting the furniture dirty.

The magic would handle it. And even if it didn't, the Beast couldn't have cared less.

"So." Bonnie chewed her lip. The Beast wished she were biting into it instead. "Let's get this over with."

The Beast curled back her lips. "Say what you mean."

"Let's see what kind of monster you are."

The Beast growled low. The words made something tingle in her blood. She'd decided long ago she could never indulge the desire she felt. But then she'd asked this human here.

And the damn fool had actually come. Had risked the

horrors of Eastvale to save someone she loved and had made her peace with the price she had to pay. Apparently.

But that doesn't mean it's me you're going to love. And I don't even know you either.

The Beast padded around her, restless. She wanted to lie down, to settle in next to her, to feel the warmth and heat of a woman, like she hadn't in so long. And then there was that other scent, that rhythm in her blood...

"You talk like you wanted to come here," the Beast snapped.

"Maybe I did."

That was so much better than "I'm just here to save someone." It was perfect. It was wonderful. It was exactly what the Beast wanted to hear.

Which meant her guest had probably rehearsed it.

Still, that would work. The Beast tore off her shirt, slicing through the rough fabric in irritated impatience and letting it fall tattered to the floor.

It didn't reveal enough. Not really. The transformation that had given her fur and claws and fangs had broadened her chest but shrunk her breasts. She didn't have a human woman's breasts any more, prominent and obvious. Instead, her fur hid rows of small nipples, like a dog's or a cat's.

She'd welcomed it at first, liked how it made it easier to hide the princess everyone had expected before she turned. She'd bound her breasts before she changed, strutted and preened before mirrors, pleased with the masculine figure it cut. But bothering with that had always been a hindrance.

Now, it seemed her own body was the problem. When Bonnie looked at her, what did she see?

Do you like women or men?

"Come over here," Bonnie said.

The Beast snarled. "You come here. You're the sacrifice."

Bonnie didn't hesitate. She got up and walked toward the Beast in the middle of the floor. Like before, she looked her over. But this time, she didn't even try to hide it. She stared down at the Beast's feet, the claws that tipped them. She lifted her head, slow and deliberate, taking in the long, loping legs again and the wide hips that becoming something more than human hadn't quite taken away. She looked at her exposed chest, covered only by her fur.

The Beast might not have a human's chest anymore, but she still remembered what it meant to be exposed. What it meant to have that part of you looked over. Her stomach fluttered with an odd embarrassment.

Bonnie stepped up to her, one lip quirked in a slight grin. Like she understood. Like she knew.

You do like this, the Beast thought.

Then Bonnie reached out and tangled her little human fingers in her fur, and the Beast forgot to think anything at all.

Bonnie's hands traced the shape of her pectorals. They found her first row of nipples, small and firm, already hardening under her touch. Under a woman's touch, when it had been so long. Bonnie laughed and took one of them between her fingers, and the Beast thought she might pull and wanted it, welcomed it, a little spike of pain that she could answer with tooth and claw and—

She's human, you damn fool.

And Bonnie's hand was moving already, her touch too light and too short. She rooted around beneath the Beast's fur, and one of her delicate human fingers slid over another of the Beast's teats. The Beast purred in spite of herself, a strangled little growl.

But Bonnie was less excited. "What—?"

"It changed me," the Beast snapped. She licked her lips in frustration. "Most animals have more than two. And don't have breasts either, not like your kind."

Your kind? She's a human, not some creature.

"Breasts?" Bonnie said.

The Beast tensed under Bonnie's touch. Would that hand withdraw now that she knew? That touch she hadn't felt in so many long years?

"I was a woman," she said at last. "But humans like you can't tell that so easily, because you're used to... well." She cast a pointed glance at Bonnie's chest, full and inviting, suddenly wishing she'd at least asked to look at her before making her confession.

Bonnie blinked. Her hand against the Beast's chest twitched. Then she laughed.

"That's a relief," she said. Then her eyes narrowed. "If anything's a relief in here."

The Beast howled with laughter of her own. *So you like monsters and women. How exactly did I manage that?*

She pulled Bonnie closer, a rough gesture that made Bonnie gasp.

"If anything's a relief in here?" the Beast mocked, dropping her voice even lower than her transformation had made it and snarling, an exaggerated, animal sound. "I don't think so."

Not bothering to offer more warning, she swept out a claw, tearing at Bonnie's dress. Those impossibly big, soft human breasts peeked out, just barely held in by her undergarment.

A simple brassiere. The Beast silently thanked the ancients for their clever clothing. Or the artisans who copied them, for pandering to rich merchants' desires for fancy things.

And there was so little here that came from the ancients, whether their expertise at craftsmanship or their mysterious machines. The enchantress who'd cursed the Beast had seen to that. The fae were the ancients' rivals, ascendant at last.

That made the brassiere even better. A secret bit of contraband snuck in by the one who was here to defy the curse. Whether she'd manage to break it or not, that came with its own little bit of satisfaction.

But whether the garment was a rare antique or a priceless copy, and whatever defiance it offered, none of that was supposed to matter to a monster. And besides, the Beast wanted her, not her garments. She ripped through the fabric with a low, guttural laugh.

"You—!" Bonnie cried, staring down at her exposed flesh,

at the tatters of her ruined garment.

"I don't know what you wanted with me when you came here, human. I don't know if you mean to convince yourself you love me. And I don't think sex is enough to lift a faerie's curse. But I know that you want this."

Bonnie bit her lip and looked down at the Beast's hand on her chest. The Beast could guess how strange it looked to a young human, clawed and furred and iridescent in the light.

She put her hand over the Beast's. "I do. I don't know if it will save you, but I do."

The Beast yipped. "Save me? Probably not."

Bonnie looked at her. The Beast spoke again, before she could. "But I don't think either of us meant to do that anyway."

Bonnie smiled, and pushed at the Beast's hand.

The Beast needed no encouragement. She slit the last clinging remnant of cloth and tore away Bonnie's ruined brassiere.

Bonnie took a gasping breath and stilled under her touch, as if she worried that those claws would tear at her. The Beast's hands twitched. She wanted them to, wanted to pierce the furless skin and feel the blood well up warm and wet from the cuts.

But she couldn't. Not with a human who didn't know her yet.

"Don't worry," the Beast soothed. "I won't cut unless you want me to."

Under her touch, Bonnie shivered again.

The Beast leaned in and nuzzled Bonnie's neck again, like she'd wanted to do again ever since she'd leaned in to smell her before.

But this time, she knew she wouldn't have to content herself with just a sniff. She rubbed the top of her furred head along Bonnie's neck, rough and possessive. She followed that up with her fangs, tracing them over the soft, delicate skin and whimpering with the effort it took to hold back.

Bonnie wrapped a hand around the Beast's head and

twined her fingers in the fur on top of it.

All right then.

The Beast nipped at her neck, just barely letting herself pierce the skin. Blood beaded up from the bite, a burst of bright vivid flavor on her tongue that reminded her just how little that cooked dinner had done to sate her hunger.

Bonnie cried out, a sharp sound that became a low keen the Beast hoped meant desire. She purred into Bonnie's neck and lapped at the wound her fangs had made.

That drew out a moan for real, long and low, deeper than the Beast recalled a human voice could be. She wrapped a hand around Bonnie's breast, feeling the soft smoothness of it, and curled her hands tight around the flesh, half hoping her claws wouldn't pierce it, half hoping for an accident she could say she didn't mean.

Bonnie's hand slid down to the fur at the back of the Beast's neck and caught there, the grip tight enough to sting. The Beast clenched her hand tighter around Bonnie's breast, tight as she dared. How much force did it take to bruise a human?

"Please," Bonnie panted, and she squeezed tighter for just a moment. Then she let go and flicked a claw over Bonnie's nipple. Bonnie gasped again and clutched her tighter.

"Please," she said again. "Get me out of this dress."

The Beast scooped her up in her arms. Cradling a human was all too easy.

"This couch, or—?"

"Let's see what kind of beds you have in here." Bonnie gave her another little smile.

This is crazy.

But that didn't really matter. The human—*Bonnie*, she told herself, *not "the human"*—was warm and restless in her arms. Her breasts bore the purple beginnings of bruises. Apparently the Beast hadn't been gentle enough. But Bonnie didn't seem to mind.

The Beast carried her to the fanciest of the bedrooms,

one she'd never bothered much with herself. Light, gauzy curtains framed the bed and draped over the windows, and fine tapestries hung on the walls. Gold thread wove through them, and they glowed with a faerie sheen.

These were the only tapestries that depicted humans, all of them beautiful, most of them women. They sat or stood near the animals, coaxing a stag into a hidden glen or touching a unicorn's horn and smiling.

The Beast had never liked them. They'd reminded her too much of the visitors she'd never have, the desire they'd never feel unless she forced their hand.

Well, now she had. And it hadn't worked out so badly after all. Maybe whatever the enchantress and her magic wanted made some sense after all. Even though she highly doubted that the enchantress understood humans, or courtship, or consent.

Light filtered in through the sheer curtains, and Bonnie looked as faerie-blessed as anyone might in their warm glow. Her hair spilled out behind her head, still bright. The Beast wondered again if she'd found someone the fae favored.

Or had it been so long since she'd bothered with a human that she was seeing magic everywhere?

She sighed and laid Bonnie down on the bed, the sound becoming a rumble of approval as she looked down. "That dress will need replacing."

"This is a big castle. If you're a woman, you either lived here or you tore the lady of the house to pieces when you turned. You'll find me a dress."

The Beast chuckled. The castle had room-sized closets filled with dresses, both the ones the Beast had never liked to wear and others the enchantress's magic had created. Courting gifts, the Beast guessed, woven of gold and silver and gossamer fiber thinner and shinier than even the cloths the ancients made with their machines.

The Beast opened all her eyes and gave Bonnie her best creature grin, not caring if she slavered. A Beast was a wild thing after all, wild and faerie-mad.

She ripped at Bonnie's dress. The fabric tore under her claws easily, too easily, reminding the Beast just how thin the skin beneath must be. She trembled with the effort of holding back, of making sure she didn't pierce it. She curled her claws inward, panting with desire and concentration.

Bonnie had no such qualms. She grabbed at torn and muddied scraps of fabric and yanked. Her breasts bounced free, and the little pad of flesh at her stomach made the Beast want to settle in against it and rip into it all at once.

"Aren't you supposed to be cursed?" Bonnie teased, pulling up a shapely leg still hidden by the last remnants of the dress.

The Beast leaned down and set upon it with her fangs. She grabbed the cloth in her long jaws and shook it, as though it were some prey-beast she meant to destroy.

Bonnie gasped at that and bit her lip, and the Beast laughed her elation through a mouthful of fabric wet with her own saliva. She raised her head, tearing the fabric as she did, and spat it out on the floor below them.

"You—" Bonnie began. But the Beast had already turned back to her, drawn by the sight of a thick thigh.

She did not think. She did not try. She did not wait to remember being human. She opened her mouth and sank her fangs into the flesh.

The coppery taste of blood filled her mouth, a vibrant benediction. Better than any prey she'd tasted, and hot with a desire no other prey could offer her.

Bonnie tensed beneath her, and she wrapped her hands around Bonnie's body to hold her still.

Did I hurt her? For real?

But Bonnie only moaned and wrapped her hands around the Beast's back, gripping hard to get her hands around it. She threw back her head with a laughing gasp. Her nails weren't sharp. Not by the Beast's standards, anyway. But their faint bite made a promise, and that was good enough.

The Beast licked at the wounds she'd made, lapping away the blood. Bonnie moaned and clutched tighter at her back, her fingers grabbing at tufts of fur.

The Beast closed her eyes, the heady taste of the blood filling her mouth and her mind. But that wasn't the only scent that filled her nostrils. She slid her head upward, drawn by another, its promise as intoxicating as the blood that already stained her lips and fangs.

A thin triangle of satiny fabric, already damp with the evidence of Bonnie's desire, hid away her sex.

"All right then," growled the Beast. She swiped out with her claws, slitting the fabric and pulling it away in one sharp gesture. But this time she didn't let her fears slow the movement.

She paused only a moment to look at the prize she'd unearthed, then ran her fingers over the slick skin. She found Bonnie's clit with one finger and turned her hand around to rub the surface of one claw over it. Bonnie gave a surprised little gasp at the sensation and then bucked her hips, wanting more.

The Beast gave an eager little purr of her own, moved her fingers away, and lowered her muzzle to Bonnie's flesh. The scent of her sex filled the Beast's nostrils, and she could smell the tang of the blood from her thigh coming after it, like an aftertaste, like a whispered promise.

Bonnie unwound her hands from the fur of the Beast's back and slid it up through the mane of hair at her neck. The Beast purred, long and low, and Bonnie's hands gripped tight around the back of her head, pushing her down.

She traced clawed fingers along Bonnie's outer labia, reminding her of their bite but not piercing the skin.

"If you move I'll pierce you," the Beast teased. Bonnie glared down at her. The Beast pressed her claw harder against the skin with a triumphant little laugh. Bonnie shivered, then froze.

Satisfied, the Beast stretched out her tongue to lick. The flesh beneath her mouth was silken-soft, softer even than the furless skin she'd caressed before. And the scent— sharp, tangy, and pure, not the wild, fierce smell of prey but something else, something gentler, something soothing she'd forgotten.

She slipped her tongue inside Bonnie, tasting her wetness, then slid free and lapped at Bonnie's clit.

Her chest rumbled in a purr. Bonnie's hand wound tight in her hair, tight and strong, and her own flesh pulsed in answer. She growled against Bonnie's flesh.

Bonnie knew better than to move, but her legs trembled with the effort to keep still. The Beast moved her claws away, and Bonnie rocked her hips hard, grinding her flesh against the Beast's muzzle. The Beast redoubled her efforts and closed her eyes, savoring the smell and scent and taste.

Bonnie mewled, a plaintive little sound. The Beast chuckled deep in her throat and wrapped her hands around Bonnie's thighs. She pushed them apart, far enough to elicit a groan from Bonnie, and held them in place with all her supernatural strength. She focused her attention on Bonnie's clit, and held Bonnie down as she twitched.

You're going to feel all of this, little human.

Bonnie writhed beneath her mouth and cried out, as if it was too much.

But in the end, she was the one who pressed the Beast's head hard against her flesh.

"So let's see you," Bonnie murmured. She stared at the Beast out of lidded eyes and stretched.

The Beast looked down at her, then at her own chest. Dark fur still covered it, and it was flat as ever.

So making a human come won't do it, then.

Bonnie didn't seem to mind. But the Beast felt oddly bashful, even as her own body ached for Bonnie's touch. The embarrassment she'd felt at Bonnie seeing her breasts was back now, stronger. The bravado she'd felt before was gone now.

Bonnie liked her shifted body. That was clear. But what if this actually worked? If she did change—if this wasn't just a strange little human, tempted by a stranger creature—would Bonnie like her less?

She tried to make a show of it, unbuttoning her pants

with practiced grace. Learning how to do that with claws had taken a while, and now at least she could show off.

But she'd never offered herself to a human before.

Oh, she'd imagined one wanting her, thousands of times. Succumbing to tooth and claw. But she'd never allowed herself the fantasy that a human would touch her back.

And now Bonnie wanted to. As before, Bonnie stared at her hips. Her gaze lingered on the Beast's furred thighs.

The Beast didn't have the curly tuft of hair a human woman had on her pubis. Instead, the fur from her belly down to her pelvis grew thicker and darker, and shone with a brighter purple sheen when the light hit it.

Well, if she was supposed to be showing off, she supposed it served well enough.

Under it, her inner labia hung down, a dusky plum color. They'd never been dainty, even before her transformation, but the shift had made her vulva big, exaggerated as any of her monstrous features.

Could Bonnie see it, under all that fur?

"Come here," Bonnie said. "Lie down with me."

The Beast made a quizzical sound deep in her throat. She'd always pictured herself above her human partner, grabbing and scratching and biting and claiming. Now Bonnie wanted her on that lacy little bed, lying down next to her like the princess she'd failed at being?

Bonnie gestured again. The Beast sighed and lay down.

The bed was soft, soft as a dream, and Bonnie was warm beside her. She wrapped her arms around the Beast and lingered for a moment, then propped herself up.

"Let's have a look at you," she said again.

But she did more than look. She pressed pink fingers to the Beast's hips and ran them over her thighs, feeling the muscles or the texture of her fur or both. The Beast closed her secondary eyes, basking in the sensation.

Bonnie, a human, a woman, was touching her, leaning down over her body with the marks of the Beast's hands and claws on her chest.

The Beast wanted to remember the sight.

Bonnie slipped a hand between the Beast's legs. The Beast shivered. Had women's touches always felt so feather-light?

Bonnie's fingers moved on the Beast's flesh, slicked themselves with her wetness and smeared it over her skin. Bonnie grabbed one of the Beast's inner lips and pulled, just enough to sting a little. The Beast growled, a low, choked sound.

"You do like this." Bonnie grinned and slid her fingers up to the Beast's clit.

The transformation had enlarged that too. Bonnie slid two fingers over the engorged flesh and the Beast's low little roar broke off in a panting sigh.

"You—" the Beast tried. But how could she even say it?

She'd dreamed of this, hoped for this. Her own hands, clawed and gnarled, were nothing like the human hands she'd missed. Someone else's hands, real and warm, touching her now.

She looked up at Bonnie's face. Not the face of some imagined woman, perfect and unreal, but of someone she'd called. Someone who'd come to her willingly.

She ground her flesh against Bonnie's hand. Bonnie moved against her faster, until she groaned, the tingling heat building within her, searing and bright.

Then Bonnie moved her fingers.

The Beast snarled in warning and loss. "If you stop now, I'll tear you apart."

But Bonnie only laughed and kept her fingers poised at the Beast's entrance. "Do you want more? Do you want this?"

The Beast blinked. Did she? Since her change, she hadn't imagined anyone doing this to her. Only herself doing this to someone else. Only herself pushing her way into warm softness, feeling the flesh yield around her fingers or spreading it wide with some device, thick enough to split some poor human apart.

A monster's tools, for a monster's pleasure.

She still wanted that now. She still wanted that from

Bonnie. Even if it meant snipping her claws.

But right now—

Now this little human had undone her. Now every nerve in her skin hummed, electric and awake. Every part of her ached for more of Bonnie's touch.

"Yes," she said, her voice a hollow rasp, nothing left in it but need.

Bonnie slipped her fingers in with a smooth, practiced motion. The Beast canted her hips to meet it.

"You've waited a long time, haven't you?" Bonnie asked, and began to move.

The Beast moved with her, her low sounds becoming yips of pleasure.

"More," she ground out, pushing back faster and harder to encourage it.

Bonnie laughed again and sped up, her brows knitting in concentration. Then she slowed. The Beast keened and licked her fangs in frustration but didn't say anything. She finally had her human, and she hadn't had to trick her to get her here.

Bonnie rewarded her patience by sliding another finger in. The Beast howled. Humans might be small and slight, but that filled her so much better.

Bonnie drove her fingers in again, harder and faster this time, all teasing forgotten. The Beast could hear her breathing hard, a human straining to match a monster's hunger.

The Beast's eyes flicked open at the sensation and she opened her mouth to say *yes, that, more,* but Bonnie's thumb thrilled over her clit and words failed her entirely.

She threw back her head with a long, rolling yelp. Bonnie pushed her fingers deeper and the Beast's flesh locked tight around her hand as a spasm of pleasure rocked her at last.

"Apparently I'm not in love with you," Bonnie said.

Was that amusement, or concern, or resignation? The Beast couldn't tell, not with the sleepy haze of pleasure making it hard to concentrate.

She blinked, her flesh still pulsing with the rhythm of

aftershock. "Do you have to be?"

She should have been disappointed. She was supposed to be disappointed. And yet, just the little taste of pleasure Bonnie had offered her had felt so good.

Bonnie glared at her. "It's your curse. You're the one who wanted to be rid of it."

She still looked perfect on the bed, her voluptuous, feminine form matching the canopied bed far better than the Beast ever had. Her hair, still eerily bright in the light, fell around her head in a gleaming curtain.

Is it enchanted? The Beast wondered again. *Or was I just hoping it would be? The woman who might save me, blessed by the same magic that cursed me?*

And she'd worn those old clothes too, wordless memories of the ancients. Testaments to all the ancients had made that the fae couldn't make with their magic and their tricks. A little hint of defiance, slipping in through Eastvale's cursed and moldy doors.

And then there were Bonnie's marks. Her bite and the drying blood a shock of red against pale flesh. The purple bruises on her chest. All a testament to what had happened here.

All a sign that, for one brief moment at least, this human had been hers.

And that she'd given herself over too. Her sex throbbed with the memory, a pleasant little burn.

She lifted her hand, turned it so that the iridescence in her palm caught the light. Then she turned it over, looked at her fur, her claws and the thick knobby shape of her knuckles.

The enchantress had meant her body to be ugly. But it had become hers. She could hear beating hearts, smell blood, feel it burst over her lips and tongue and teeth. She could run faster and jump farther than she had ever imagined as a human.

And she'd come to love her solitude.

"I wanted someone to come here," she said at last. "I wanted to know if someone would come for me."

"By making a threat."

The Beast rumbled low in her throat, not sure if what she felt was indignation or shame. "I told you before. Faerie magic isn't fair."

"No, it isn't. It never has been. I already know that."

The Beast sighed. "Then let me say what I wanted to say."

Bonnie looked at the Beast for a long moment. She worried her lip with her teeth. "Go ahead," she said at last.

"I wanted someone to come here. To try to break my curse, yes. But I don't know if I wanted them to succeed."

Bonnie propped herself up on her arms. "Well then."

The Beast hung her head. Maybe she did feel ashamed, after all. "I never should have called you here."

"You never should have threatened anyone," Bonnie agreed. "Not my father and not me. But he told me what waited. What happened between you. What you were."

The Beast's only answer was another low growl.

"I came here of my own will. And if you think I didn't want you, you haven't been paying attention."

The Beast's rumble became a low purr that shook her whole chest.

Bonnie reached down to touch it and grinned. "Besides, the fae don't always get things right."

The Beast yipped with laughter. "They don't understand humans. I don't think they ever did."

"And you do?"

"I was human once. They never were. But there's plenty I've forgotten."

"There's plenty you don't know about the fae either." Those full, pouty lips quirked into a mocking little grin that made the Beast want to bite them.

"Or just that you don't realize," Bonnie went on. "I can see why some faerie thought you were a fool."

The Beast lunged and snapped before she realized she had done it. Her jaws closed inches from Bonnie's face. "Don't," she snarled, her voice all roar.

Bonnie blinked, but didn't move. "Do you think you're

the only one who's dealt with faeries?"

The Beast's jaws worked. She slavered, angry. Bonnie ignored it.

"What are you saying?" The Beast snarled. Then she blinked in dawning comprehension. "Your hair."

Bonnie nodded. "Are you done trying to attack me now?"

The Beast hung her head, abashed.

"My faerie godmother's blessing didn't always give me what I wanted," Bonnie said. "Why shouldn't your curse give you what you do want sometimes?"

"Then I was right. They did give you a gift."

Now it was Bonnie's turn to laugh. "Do you think you're the first unfortunate soul someone hoped I would save? People notice."

"So how did you—?"

Bonnie reached out her hand and pressed her fingers to the Beast's muzzle, apparently fearless despite the Beast snapping at her just moments ago. "Shh."

The Beast couldn't resist. She nipped at Bonnie's fingers hard enough to make Bonnie yelp in surprise and pain.

It felt good.

"Tell me," the Beast said.

"I plan to."

The Beast tilted her head. "You plan to?"

"Eventually, yes." Bonnie's smile deepened. "I was supposed to break your curse. I haven't done that yet."

The Beast's primary eyes widened. "You want to stay here? With me?"

Bonnie nodded. "As long as I can tell my father I haven't been devoured by an evil monster, why not?"

"You have no reason to stay. Not anymore." Her chest rumbled. "You're not going to save me."

"Who says I have to save you to stay?"

The Beast's eyes widened again. Then she laughed, low and deep. "No one."

Bonnie winked. "Then we have time. Time for stories. Yours and mine."

The Beast rumbled. Tell her story? Tell Bonnie all about the arrogant little fool she'd been, finally having a castle to herself and the power to do what she wanted with it?

"I might even tell you my name someday," Bonnie whispered, quiet and intimate.

She wrapped her hands around the back of the Beast's head. Her fingers tangled in the fur there. Slowly, she brought the Beast's head down to rest on the soft pillows of her chest.

The Beast settled against them, purring again.

COURTING THE FLAME

MOST PEOPLE thought Jon Hayes was a vampire. Most people were wrong.

The mistake was understandable. All kinds of creatures prowled the city, especially at night, and Jon did his best to look the part.

He'd always liked velvet and frills, even if the other humans thought he looked pretentious. It wasn't his fault he'd been born in the wrong century.

And he wasn't dressing for them, anyway. He wore what he had to at work, came home at night, and slipped into the costumes that made him feel like more than what he was. Made him feel like one of the monsters. Like he could stalk the streets after the sun went down, instead of being ready to run.

His apartment had too many mirrors. Pointless, if he wanted to become a vampire. But the men he brought home were usually too dazzled to mind. And if you were going to collect fancy clothes, you might as well look at your reflection. If you had to be some boring, humdrum human, you might as well enjoy it when you could.

When Jon slipped into a ruffled shirt, pouted his thick lips, and held a glass of red wine by its delicate stem, he could almost believe. Could almost believe that his dull little apartment was a room in a tall mansion, overlooking the city. Could almost believe that the people rushing by five floors below were his prey, not his peers. Could almost believe that he was one of the hunters.

Or that they might come looking for him.

Vampires were picky creatures, so everyone said. Most were hundreds of years old. Some were thousands. Very few had time to bother with young humans who wanted to be sired.

But if he impressed them enough, he might just catch their attention. And prove himself worth more than a night's meal.

So he filled his apartment with musty old books that cost half a month's pay and pored over any lore he could find. He'd bought clothes, furniture, and drapes that cost still more. Rich as he looked, he subsisted on cheap meals and rarely went out.

He'd never minded. He'd known they would find him eventually.

Once they did, he'd have eternity to make it all up. And would never need to bother with instant soup again.

Or so he'd always thought.

But now, looking at the man—*or monster*, Jon reminded himself—that had just walked in, it all seemed a little silly.

The man was tall, broad-shouldered, and well-muscled enough that Jon couldn't help but grin in appreciation. He had dark brown skin and wore his hair in dreadlocks, gathered in a ponytail. Hints of gray silvered a few of his locks.

Jon's grin became a scowl. A ponytail, gathered together by some worn, misshapen band. How could an immortal dress like that? It was like he didn't even care.

At least he has enough sense to wear black, Jon thought. Still, the tight shirt, loose pants, and tall boots made him look more ready for a fight than for a night out seducing and draining humans, and Jon saw a knife at his hip.

A black tattoo peeked out from under one sleeve. The elaborate design most likely indicated which clan he came from.

If he really was a vampire.

Jon had studied the symbols and signs in his books. He knew the mark of the clan he'd called to, and he'd pored over variations and possible modifications so no variation would surprise him. But the sharp black swirls on the man's bicep didn't look much like the sigils he knew.

Maybe, if he squinted.

If he wasn't a vampire, it might still be a ward. Protection from werewolves or revenants.

Which might be promising anyway. Even if he wasn't a vampire, he might know things. Most musclemen didn't. Or if they did, they bragged about fights with the creatures of the night.

Right.

"Jonathan Hayes," the man said.

He had a deep voice, smooth and rich enough to make him grin again. But it wasn't a movie-villain voice. Wasn't a voice that would have stopped him short if he'd heard this man call out on a dark street at night.

But something hid behind his words. An echo, a little hiss, a cold and sibilant sound. Jon's heart beat faster.

It made him think of graves, graves and death and cold. But he'd been waiting for this moment for so long he might have made it all up.

What was a vampire supposed to sound like?

He twisted a ring on one of his fingers, hoping it didn't make his excitement too obvious. "And you are?"

Jon glanced at his lips, but his mouth was closed. Jon couldn't see his teeth to tell whether they were pointed or long. Jon looked down at his hands. His nails were filed to subtle points, sharp enough to send a little shiver down Jon's spine.

The man chuckled and extended a hand. "My name is

Brian."

Jon couldn't help himself. He raised an eyebrow. "Brian."

"You have a problem with my name?"

"Just Brian?"

Brian let his hand drop. Jon winced. He should have shaken it.

"You know my clan already," Brian said.

"Of course. I've taken great care to—"

"Or maybe you don't. But if you don't, you're an even bigger fool than you look."

"Bloodflame." Jon kept his voice as smooth as he could. "But when I called to them, I have to say I expected something a little... different."

Brian glared at him. "I know what you expected."

"I meant no disrespect. It's just that the Bloodflame lineage goes back almost a thousand years."

"Longer."

"Yes. Well. I thought that a representative of such an ancient clan would—"

"Would be skinny, anemic, and paler than you."

Shit.

Jon winced and lowered his head. "I—"

"If you've read enough of those books on your shelves to figure out which are worth keeping, you know you're lucky anyone answered your call."

"Of course." Jon swept a hand in front of his chest. "I'm sorry for any... unfortunate assumptions I might have made."

Brian chuckled. "You have no idea."

"And you're going to teach me?"

"Humans who try to get a vampire's attention are fools." He flashed a white-toothed grin, long enough for Jon to catch a glimpse of sharp canines but not long enough to tell if they were true fangs. "Or looking to get eaten."

Well.

"But," Jon began, "you haven't threatened me at all. Whoever you are, and whatever your rank within your clan, you seem perfectly happy to be here."

Warming to his topic, Jon allowed himself a smirk. "So I hope you can understand why I might wonder."

Brian didn't answer. With a heavy thud of boots, he marched over to the biggest of Jon's mirrors, a full-length one framed by tarnished curlicues of ornate bronze.

With a sigh of resignation—and a tingling little thrill under his skin—Jon followed.

And saw only his own elaborately dressed reflection staring back at him.

Jon polished the glass himself, eased away every streak with aching fingers weekly at least. He stood in front of it all the time, inspecting his reflection before he went out into the haunted night. Smoothing back his blond hair and taming wayward strands. Fixing collars, smoothing wrinkles. Practicing the perfect pout. He had to keep his mirror perfect.

People didn't just not show up in a mirror like that.

"So you are real," Jon whispered. Overcome, he stared at his own image in the glass.

His eyes passed over the frills of his shirt, the rich brocaded purple of his vest. He'd wanted to wear a jacket, something velvet-soft and dark, but it was too warm for that.

And getting worse, with Brian here. Even his vest felt thick and heavy, and he sweated too much under it.

Rings adorned his fingers and a pendant hung around his neck. The gem in it glittered, iridescent red. He'd always loved the way it looked, but next to Brian the color felt clichéd.

It was a summoning-stone. *Or so the books said.* He scowled, remembering what Brian had said about them. Which books were worth keeping? The man standing beside him could tell him.

If he had enough to offer.

He thought he had. He thought he'd made sure of it. But he'd expected an aristocrat, not... Brian. He took a deep breath and looked at himself a moment longer, for lack of anything better to do.

His pants were black. Black and too boring. His favorites still needed to be cleaned. His boots made up for it, at least.

They gleamed with the effort he'd taken to polish them.

He'd done it himself, of course. He would have had someone else do it, if he could've. It would have felt right, dressed in his finery. It would have meant someone below him, tending to him, looking up now and then and wondering just who and what he was.

He did exactly that sometimes. When he could afford the luxury. He liked it. They saw his clothes and his manner and did what he wanted, as quickly as they could. He might have been a vampire, after all.

But this time around he hadn't had the cash for that kind of indulgence. So he'd done it himself, as soon as he'd heard the answer to his summons. His arms ached, remembering it.

And next to him stood Brian the reflectionless, wearing street clothes, his dreadlocks held together with a cheap little band.

He'd dressed better than the vampire. Should that make him feel foolish or superior? He looked over at Brian's shoulder—solid and real and broad with muscle, now that he wasn't looking in the mirror.

If Brian had bothered to come here, something must have impressed him. He grinned at his own reflection, reached up to run a ring-festooned hand through his blond, wavy hair.

"Are you done preening?" Brian asked, those strange, low vibrations thrilling through his voice.

They mean you're interested, don't they?

Jon kept his eyes on his reflection. As long as he stared at himself, Brian would be too.

"Are you done looking?" he returned, and watched himself laugh.

Brian laughed, deep and rich. "Maybe not," he said to Jon's reflection.

Jon turned. He had to. He couldn't stand it anymore, not seeing Brian's face, not knowing if his guest—*his vampire*—was laughing at him or finally ready to play the game at last.

"Then maybe we have better things to do than stand in front of the mirror," Jon said.

At least now they were in the bedroom.

Jon's hands tightened into fists at his sides. He glared at Brian, who sat on his bed with his legs dangling down.

This isn't what I meant.

Brian had sat down as soon as they came inside, still wearing those depressingly plain clothes, and asked for a glass of water. Like a friend sitting down for a chat. In the middle of a room with blood-plum painted walls, with the best books culled from ancient grimoires sitting in a pile on the nightstand next to him.

And he was a vampire, the vampire Jon had always wanted. Just sitting on the bed, like there wasn't enough space to sit down in the other room, instead of pulling off his clothes or shoving Jon down onto it and—

Water. It was absurd. Vampires hunted humans and drained their blood in the night. What would they want with water? Jon had felt so insulted he'd poured it lukewarm from the tap and handed it to Brian in his plainest glass.

But Brian only raised an eyebrow and drank. Deep. Too deep. Jon watched his throat move, shivered, and slipped out of the vest. Maybe he could still make something of this.

That earned him a chuckle, low and cold and rich.

"Why water?" Jon snapped, too irritated to let himself savor the attention.

"Blood is mostly water," Brian said, the laugh still in his voice. "Why are you so surprised?"

Jon narrowed his eyes. "Are you telling me you already ate?"

"Do you hope I did, or hope I didn't?" Brian looked straight at him and smiled. Dark lips spread apart in a slow smile. His teeth gleamed. And the sharp jut of the canines made Jon flush.

He squirmed, his pants beginning to feel tight. But he'd been waiting for this moment, and he wasn't about to let a water-drinking vampire fluster him. "I told you before. I'm hoping you'll turn me. Not kill me."

Brian looked directly at Jon's hips. "Or something else."

"Or something else." Jon shot Brian another impish little grin and undid the first few buttons of his shirt. "But why tell me what you are if that's all you want?" He looked Brian up and down, puckered his lips in a mocking kiss. "You could've had that anyway."

"You're the one who wanted more than that."

Brian stared at Jon. His gaze trailed upward.

Toward Jon's neck. That at least made sense.

Brian laughed. His tongue darted out to lick his teeth.

Jon swallowed hard, thought of Brian watching his Adam's apple bob up and down.

What had Brian said before? *Skinny, anemic, and pale?*

It didn't seem to be a problem for him now. Now he stared at Jon, eyes wide and unblinking. Jon stared back for as long as he could.

He blinked. His eyes burned, even after doing it. "You insulted my apartment, my body, my books, my knowledge. After all that" —he tilted his hips in invitation or mockery or both—"is this how I'm supposed to prove myself to you?"

Brian snickered. Jon shuddered again and squirmed.

"It's how you want to try," Brian said.

Jon's mouth twisted into a sour little scowl.

Brian set the water glass down without looking. Too quickly and too loudly.

Jon shivered again. How strong were those muscle-thick arms? And how much of that strength came from whatever workouts vampires did, and how much from hunting, and how much from the dark magic that gave them their unlife?

Jon slipped off his shirt and let it fall, a white bird of fabric fluttering down to land at his feet. He slid it aside with his heel, still looking back at Brian.

He had to take off his boots. He pouted and slid his fingers down to the laces. He kept his gaze fixed on Brian for as long as he could and untied them, only gave up when he had to blink.

When he looked back up, Brian was lounging on the bed.

Getting comfortable? Jon stood up straight again and tried not to gloat.

His hands moved down to his waist, unbuttoned the first button of his fly with as much deliberate care as he could stand. Under the fabric, cocooned in his briefs, his cock bulged with an aching heat.

He stopped, his fingers curled around the fabric.

"You too," he made himself say, trying for the saucy purr he'd practiced countless times in front of too many mirrors.

Brian raised an eyebrow. He was still looking at Jon, and maybe he still hadn't blinked. But the gesture looked so ordinary Jon almost laughed again.

"I want to see you, too," he said.

"You're making demands?"

That voice again, the snake-hiss hidden under it. Jon closed his eyes and tried not to drown.

"*You're* drinking water. You didn't answer when I asked if... if you fed. You'll kill me if I don't impress you. Isn't that what you want me to think?"

Brian didn't answer.

Jon fought the urge to move his hands. He gripped the fabric until it hurt, closed his eyes, and ignored the heat and pressure just below his fingertips. "It's only fair I get to ask for something."

Brian smiled, a toothy, hungry grin. He slipped off his shirt.

Brian was beautiful, just like he'd expected. Too beautiful for clothes faded and ragged with use, for simple, tied-back hair. Too beautiful to feel real.

Jon had expected more tattoos to go with the Bloodflame symbol on Brian's bicep. Wards. Protections, showing what kinds of monsters vampires feared or fought with. Symbols of rank within his clan. How long ago they'd turned him. How many of those thousands of years of clan history he'd lived to see.

Jon wouldn't know what all the tattoos meant. Meeting Brian made it painfully clear just how little he knew and how much he'd assumed. But at least he'd know more than he knew now. At least he could guess at Brian's age, or his rank, or his purpose.

Whether he recruited humans, or just felt like having sex with one tonight. Jon snickered.

But he only saw one other mark on Brian's skin. A raised scar on his chest, a teardrop-shaped flame. The clan symbol again, Jon supposed. But it must mean something the tattoo didn't. Otherwise, why bother with both? Jon glared at the books on his nightstand.

Not enough. Never enough.

Whatever the scar meant, he liked it. Pattern or not, it proved Brian was human once. Proved that he could touch, kiss, taste.

"Is that enough for you?" Brian teased, looking at his hands.

"No."

Jon licked his own lips. Prey throwing a threat back in his predator's face.

It felt good.

Brian growled. The sound echoed, hollow and cold. Jon froze, his chest bare and his pants half unbuttoned. Something told him to run but he couldn't. Didn't know how. Didn't want to.

Deer in the headlights. He forced himself to blink. His eyelids felt locked in place, the muscle movement a terrible effort.

But when he looked at Brian again, he only saw Brian slip off his clothes, then turn to him and wink. Big dusty boots sitting at the edge of the bed. All perfectly ordinary. Like anyone he might bring home.

He leaned closer, eyes wide. Brian shook his head. Probably too obvious, but Jon couldn't help himself. His books said plenty of interesting things about the virile members of monsters and demons, but very little about vampires. Only about their appetites, for almost everyone.

He found himself a little disappointed.

He didn't know what he expected. Sparkles? Barbs? Some kind of sharp, dangerous shape? But whatever perfect proportions Brian's transformation had given him, his cock looked perfectly normal. Invitingly hard—and Jon felt his own twitch in response—but otherwise just like anyone else.

Jon tried not to snicker. But he did allow himself a crooked little smile. Brian would take it as an invitation anyway. Which was fine. Jon didn't want him any less. He just liked having his own little secret.

He undid the last button with deliberate, obscene care. Let his pants fall and his underwear with them. Brian might like the show—did, if that stare meant he wasn't just hungry—but if he really was a thousand years old he'd seen stripteases before.

Jon slinked over to the bed with his best sashaying walk. Brian still didn't blink, his eyes eerily open. Jon leaned over him, emboldened.

"Prove myself?" he purred. "I guess that means I'm the one seducing y—*ahhh!*"

Strong arms seized him. Their grip tightened around him, heavy and immovable as stone, and Brian flipped him over before he even knew Brian had lunged for him. He stared up at the ceiling, the yellow and flickering light of an old fixture he'd always wanted to change glaring down at him.

He sank into the impossible softness of too-expensive, satiny sheets. They felt good. Or would have if his ribs weren't aching with the memory of Brian's inhuman grip.

But neither mattered much to Jon. Not the pain in his ribs or the billowing pleasure of the sheets against his back.

He felt nothing but the cold.

If Brian had just touched him—tapped his shoulder, shaken his hand—he might not have noticed. Might have thought Brian's fingers were clammy or the night outside was cold. That his guest still needed time to warm up.

But Brian was a vampire, and Jon had made it his business years ago to know about the creatures of the night. He'd raised himself on tales of witches' wintry teats, of demons' frozen emissions chilling mortals from the inside.

And even without those stories, it made sense. Brian was dead. Or something like it.

Jon shivered. From the chill of Brian's lifeless skin against his living heat. From fear. From expectation. From knowledge deep down in his flesh now, where his mind couldn't wonder any more.

He wrapped his hands around Brian's back and pressed his palms against the cool smoothness of his skin. His fingers found another scar. Not a symbol or a design, but the jagged slash of some long-ago violence.

Right. You were human once.

He clenched his hands into claws, dug in hard enough to scratch with his fingernails.

He had what he wanted. What he'd been looking for all his life.

Or it had him.

"Is this what you wanted?" Brian's face above him teased, the dreadlocks hanging down around it. "Is this what you thought I would do?"

Brian leaned down. Jon felt breath on his neck, a memory of winter nights, puffs of steam in the cold air. He arched his neck and laughed, slid his knee up just to feel Brian's leg against his and shiver at the chill.

Brian's mouth pressed against Jon's neck. Jon waited, still again, held by some strange hypnosis. Brian's lips parted, slow and deliberate. The tips of his fangs pricked Jon's skin. Small drops of blood beaded up from the cuts.

Jon twitched, even as heat shimmered through his body, a warmth that started in the tiny wounds Brian's fangs had made and pooled in his straining cock.

"I—" Jon said, his voice like molasses in his throat. He moved his hand to Brian's chest with a child's slow, awkward movements.

His fingers slipped over the teardrop scar. He clutched at it. The texture of it grounded him.

His other hand moved to Brian's neck. He was only

human. Could never push a vampire away. And the dreaming in his veins meant he didn't want to anyway. He'd wanted something, but he couldn't remember what it was. What more was there than this?

He'd been looking for something. Something else.

"I want—" he whispered. "I want—"

Brian laughed against his skin.

"I want you to turn me," Jon whispered at last. "Not kill me."

Brian chuckled. Jon felt his mouth open and close. His tongue lapped at the tiny cuts.

It was Jon's turn to laugh, a choked, giddy sound. "You do like me."

His hands slipped around Brian's back and down to his ass. He pressed Brian closer, arched his hips, his cock against Brian's chilled flesh.

Brian gasped. His cool breath stung the cuts on Jon's neck.

Jon reached down and slipped his hand between them. He curled his fingers around Brian's cock. It stayed cold. Brian's eyes closed.

"You're warm," Brian said, his voice ragged. "Like any human."

Jon arched his hips and wriggled, pushing as much of his skin against Brian's as he could. Brian twitched his hands. *Living warmth*, Jon thought, and snickered.

"Any human? Is this what you do with all of us? Hold out the hope of turning us, just so you can feel our heat?"

Brian laughed again. The shadows danced to the sound of his voice. "I've lived for over a century. Do you really think I chase after humans just because I'm cold?"

"You don't miss being human, then? Your life—unlife—whatever—isn't all loneliness and despair?"

"Miss being human? Would you?"

Jon raised an eyebrow. Brian didn't answer.

Ignoring me again.

His hand moved to Brian's face. The rough beginnings of

stubble scraped against his fingers. He wrapped a hand around Brian's chin.

He wondered, for a moment, if Brian would let him move it. Or if, like any good monster, he'd keep his eyes fixed on the real prize. But when he drew Brian's head up, toward his face, the monster didn't resist.

"I think you like something," Jon breathed in his best sultry voice. "If it's not human warmth, it must be me."

The vampire's lips were rough against his. Chapped, like anyone else's might be. That was so normal, so average, so much like any other big guy with a rubber band in his hair and faded clothes.

But the strange, clammy touch of those lips was not. Chapped or no, Jon shivered at their promise. Death—but life after.

The endless life of a hunter. The life he'd always wanted. He opened his mouth and moaned.

Brian purred, a low, deep sound, rich and resonant and not quite human. His fangs worried Jon's lips. Then they bit, a sharp silvery sting, and Jon felt the wet heat of his own blood beginning to drop from his wounds.

Brian sucked at the wounds with unnatural strength and Jon stilled again. Not because of Brian's glamor shimmering through his veins. Because he had no other defense. Because Brian was a hunter, and he was helpless prey. Whatever his mind wanted, his body knew it.

There's no use in playing dead, he told it. *You win now or you lose.*

But Brian drew back and licked at the wounds, a lover's tease. The low sepulcher sound reverberated from his throat again.

I knew it! Jon thought, exultant. But he sighed with relief anyway.

He wrapped his legs around Brian, his own little gesture of possession. Brian drew his head away and stared down at him, his dark eyes bright, his lips, chin and fangs smeared with Jon's blood.

Jon answered with a wild laugh. "The lube is in the nightstand."

He would have said it to anyone he brought home, any man he'd forget in the morning. And Brian reached a dark hand to rummage in a drawer, like anyone who wasn't dead and hadn't just bit holes in Jon's lips and sucked blood out of the wounds. Jon wasn't sure if that was reassuring or ridiculous.

Brian pulled out a condom and tore open the wrapper. Jon's eyes widened.

"I want you to turn me," he said. "There's nothing for me to be afraid of. And you're already drinking my blood."

Brian snickered and rolled the condom onto his cock. "You want me to turn you." He rubbed a lube-smeared fist up and down his length. "But I haven't decided."

"You've decided not to kill me."

"Have I?"

Jon poked at the wounds in his lip with his tongue. Pain blossomed in them, sharp and welcome. Jon's hips tilted, half in response to the sting and half to offer Brian a better angle.

Brian didn't look down. His dark unblinking gaze stayed fixed on Jon's cuts and Jon's tongue licking at them. He slid himself into position without bothering to look away.

Once a monster, always a monster. Jon wrapped his legs tighter around Brian's broad frame.

His vampire slipped inside him with deliberate grace. Jon hadn't expected it, not from someone so big, someone who growled at him with a monster's voice.

But he had expected it from the vampire he'd wanted—the pale skinny aristocrat he'd thought would come for him. *Centuries of practice,* he thought. He opened his bloody mouth wide and moaned.

The low supernatural hum rumbled from Brian's throat again, too eerie for a growl. His hands moved to Jon's chest and kneaded his skin, his sharpened nails piercing new wounds there.

"Please," Jon said, and canted his hips again. His own

dick throbbed and he wanted to touch it, take it in his hands just so he could feel more.

But this was the first time a vampire answered him. The first time his dreams had finally found him. He could touch himself next time, if he wanted.

If there was one.

Brian pushed in deeper, a slow movement that woke every nerve in Jon's flesh. He moaned again, louder, half for real and half to impress his monster. To catch and hold him, now that he was here, was real, with Jon's blood on his mouth and his fingers and his cock shoved deep inside him.

Brian began to move, still careful, still deliberate. His sharpened fingertips dug deeper into Jon's skin. Blood beaded up from the cuts on Jon's chest and flowed down. Jon whimpered, a soft little sound.

He hated hearing it. It wasn't a moan, or a purr, or a plea. It was a helpless mewl. But the way Brian made him bleed drew it out of him anyway.

Brian pulled back, his hands still cat-kneading Jon's skin. He plunged in again, hard and fast, dark eyes still wide open, fangs bared in a greedy, feral snarl.

Jon threw back his head, exposed the pinpricks Brian had made in his neck, shifted to open his legs wider. His dick twitched and his precum smeared the skin underneath it.

"More," he spat through bloodied lips.

Brian gave it. Ageless finesse gone, he battered into Jon over and over. A titan's iron strength propelled him, something more than the muscles Jon's fingers clutched at his back.

Sweat slicked Brian's skin, even though the exertion hadn't warmed it. He still felt cold to Jon's touch. Jon pressed his palms to Brian's back again, and Brian growled and moved even faster.

Jon pushed out his hips, over and over, trying to move with the cock cleaving him, but it was all he could do to try to keep up. His moans died in his too-exposed throat, faded to rough panting gasps that said only Yes. Yes. *I want this. I want this. I've been waiting.*

What Brian felt, he didn't know. Wasn't sure he cared. He forgot about the condom too, the disappointment, the backhanded admission that his vampire was still hedging his bets. The driving rhythm, the speed, how deep it reached inside him—only those things mattered.

And they meant Brian needed this, too. Jon laughed up at him.

The frantic rhythm stilled. Brian hung poised above him, hips pulled back and ready to plunge in. His strange cold sweat wet Jon's palms.

Decide, Jon thought, and arched his neck again to taunt his fate and his vampire alike.

He never saw the movement. Brian sank into him, all fire and bliss, and he thrust his hips up to impale himself harder, driven by instinct alone.

Fangs tore through the skin of his throat like paper, ripping open the wounds they'd already made. Warm blood surged from the wounds even as his cock surged and spasmed, flooding his own flesh with sticky heat.

His hips rocked to the rhythm of the suction, and his heartbeat slowed. Honeyed contentment flowed through his veins, and it meant nothing at all to—

Offer it.

His eyes widened. He stared up at his too-dull ceiling with a horror that made his wounds burn, despite Brian's soothing balm.

"You—!" he tried to say, but his voice had faded away. He tilted his head as best he could toward Brian's ear and hissed something that should have been a ward but came out only as a shapeless curse, as old as hapless humans who'd been tempted and betrayed.

Brian rumbled, a hollow, echoing sound.

And drew his head away.

Blood spattered his lips and chin, smeared his white fangs red. It shouldn't have been beautiful. Brian wasn't some aristocrat savoring his meal, a secret pleasure curling his lips.

His mouth was a predator's maw, smeared with the gore of its latest kill. It looked like hunger, and craving, and death.

Jon's wound throbbed. But in his haze, or his dreams, or the hope that carried him this far, he couldn't stop himself from staring.

"You stopped," he croaked with a dying man's breath.

The dark wolf-mouth twisted into a smile. "You noticed."

Jon smirked.

Brian reached up toward his own chest. Sharpened fingernails raked over the flesh there and dug deep. Jon watched, hypnotized, as dark red blood beaded up and dripped down from the wound.

Brian was still smiling. He leaned down over Jon, and his deep too-many-voices laughed in mockery and welcome. "Drink, if you really know what you want."

Jon tilted his head up. Pain flared through his wound. He paid it no mind. It meant he'd earned this, after all.

He pressed his mouth to Brian's wound and drank.

THUNDER

THE LIGHTNING followed her.

Kay reached up and ran a hand through close-cropped hair. The storm wasn't here yet, and the soft fuzz on her head was still dry. But she could see the flashes, hear the thunder roll far off. And the sky smelled like something was coming.

And she had that old familiar feeling, the one behind her eyes, electric and crackling.

She'd thought, when she was a small child, that it meant she had powers, like a character in a cartoon. She'd waited, one overcast day when she could smell the rain coming, sure the bullies would have no idea what they were in for. She'd waited for them to taunt and tease. Call her a boy, call her confused, call her everything they came up with when they didn't feel like leaving her alone.

She'd even closed her eyes to build the drama. Run the risk of a punch or a tackle, just to make sure it was really frightening.

She'd taken a deep breath and opened them again, hoped crackling, electric light would sear them.

But it didn't work that way.

She'd known enough to take off running. To rush into the woods and not slow down. She'd only stopped when her knees buckled underneath her. She'd fallen onto a paved trail, looked up, and cursed a dark sky that hadn't kept its promise.

And just then, the lightning had struck. Downed a tree, so they couldn't follow. And she'd learned that the storms would protect her... but only as long as she followed the rules.

She'd had to earn everything: the muscles on her arms, the short crop of her hair. Sometimes with words, sometimes with fists, sometimes with the set of her shoulders and the curl of her unpainted lips.

Just like that little saying: God helps those that help themselves. Whatever gods or powers or magic watched out for her, she had to impress it first. Had to make sure the storm was with her.

It wasn't always about danger. Sometimes she wanted them, and they came.

She wanted this one. She was on her way to visit Shana.

And this one was with her, coming up after her, following her feet. She could almost see the slickness on the pavement, even though it wasn't raining yet.

She felt good. Put her arms down, squared her shoulders. She was packing, too, and she didn't always do that either. But the storm was with her today, and that made it easy to be as fearless as she tried to look.

Besides, Shana's apartment wasn't far.

Something crackled behind her eyes again. Lightning lit the sky, somewhere close, and she heard a rumble. She thought of Shana's lips and hands and smiled.

She waited until she got to the right building before she looked for the color in her eyes. Shana was the one who'd always seen it, after all.

She squinted. Looked for the brightest reflection she could find. Studied the close-crop of her hair, the low curl of her brows.

And under them, gray eyes, not quite colorful enough to be blue. That had always reminded Kay of storms anyway. But the magic, or the power, or whatever it was? That she couldn't see, not usually. She turned her head, watched herself move. She glimpsed something silvery, like a fish swimming past in the creek she'd played in as a child. But like those darting fish, the silver was gone as soon as she saw it.

It never left for Shana. Shana could always see it, glittering there in Kay's eyes. And her face always crinkled into the same smile, and she always said the same thing.

"Ninety percent chance of rain."

Kay always answered, "Ninety?"

And Shana always laughed and said, "You never know, they might change their mind."

Kay had joked, once, that there was something about femmes. That of course Shana would see it every time. That femmes liked color, liked glitter, liked glamour, and Kay just didn't know enough about that stuff. But that was bullshit, and Kay and Shana both knew it.

Kay looked up at the sky. *What do you want today?* She asked it. *I'm just going to see Shana.*

She made it halfway to the door when the thunder crashed again and the overfull sky finally let go.

The rain fell, sudden and ferocious, a flood of forceful heavy drops that drenched Kay where she stood.

"Fine," Kay muttered, trying not to crack a smile. At least it was summer and warm, not freezing cold. Her jacket would need a drying out, though, and so would the rest of her clothes.

She squared her jaw and gestured. The storm answered, a sudden, too-loud thunderclap and a blaze of bright lightning that lit the whole sky.

Kay tugged the door open and headed toward the elevator with steps she had to fight to slow.

The elevator was old, and creaked, and smelled. The rain only made the must worse. Kay didn't mind, and leaned against the wall to prove how much she didn't.

Shana was smiling, tanned face dimpled, dark eyes bright.

Kay had never seen any magic in them. But she almost never saw her own, so it stood to reason she might miss it in someone else, too.

And anyone who could look at Kay and know had to have a little bit of magic in her, too.

The curly frizz of hair that framed Shana's face was dry. So was her bright red blouse, and the matching skirt that clung to her hips. They were narrow, maybe, on someone so reedy and tall. But Kay had never minded.

Kay lingered in the door, not sure if the dry apartment looked like a luxury or a letdown. Part of her wanted to come in, to let the warm room and the warm woman within ease the water off of her.

Part of her wanted to drag Shana outside and kiss her until they both drowned.

Shana looked over Kay's shoulder, at the still-pouring sky. "You didn't need to do that. I already knew you were coming."

Kay stepped inside. She peeled off her jacket and unlaced her boots, which were already dripping. "What gave it away?"

Shana tilted her head and smiled, her face a map of smiling wrinkles. She whisked away the jacket before Kay could protest and stuck it on a rack. It was dripping too, but a towel already lay on the floor.

They'd been together for over a year now. There were towels almost everywhere.

"Let's see," Shana was saying. "How'd I know you might be coming over? I don't know."

She pursed red-painted lips. Kay thought of kissing her. "Maybe the lightning. Maybe the giant sheet of rain that just came down with no warning at all."

Kay shrugged.

"You could at least try to be subtle."

Kay answered with another thunderclap.

"They weren't even forecasting anything." Shana reached out, slipped her hand under the fabric of Kay's unbuttoned shirt. "And there you go lighting up the sky."

Shana's fingers were warm and slender. Manicured nails—red like her blouse and her lips—traced one of the tattoos on Kay's skin.

Kay let out a long breath. She'd earned those too.

And only one of them had anything to do with lightning. That was Zeus, throwing a bolt of thunder from his place on her right shoulder, just because it hadn't seemed right to leave him out. The rest were monsters, creatures, ghosts. A phoenix and a dragon on her upper arms, to celebrate the work she'd put into sculpting them.

"Don't tell me you hit a tree," Shana said. She laughed and leaned closer.

Kay slipped her fingers under Shana's chin and drew her head up. "Maybe this city needs some fire."

She didn't wait for an answer. She kissed Shana hard, rough and insistent. Heat curled through her body, another burst of lightning that wanted setting free.

She wrapped her other arm around Shana, who trembled a little in her tightening grip. But her arms, slender as they were, wrapped around Kay with a grip as tight as her own.

Shana's mouth opened, wide and hungry.

The rain came down harder, louder, rattled the blinds. Shana kissed her neck, slid her hands down, opened the buttons of Kay's shirt.

She didn't move to slide it off, not at first. She traced the shape of Kay's shoulder muscles, slid her fingertips over the remembered shapes of Kay's tattoos, and dipped her fingers into the hollow of Kay's collarbone and throat.

She pulled away just long enough to stare down at Kay's water-darkened jeans, at the telltale shape tucked away in them.

"You've got something for me," she said.

Lightning flashed.

"How long have you been walking around with that on, just for me?"

Then came the thunder, long, low, and rolling.

They didn't make it into the bedroom.

They left the blinds as open as they wanted. Shana only lived on the third floor, but there were trees near the window, and the force of the storm would make them impossible to see anyway through all the rain.

Kay pushed Shana down onto the couch with a growl of thunder. Shana laughed, a fey, free sound. The rain picked up, lashed at the windows, made them rattle. Kay leaned down over Shana and she shuddered.

Was she playing? Pretending fear to make this better? She'd known Kay a long time, and storms held no terror for her. But she could see Kay's magic. Could she sense the thing gathering inside her, the heat and the energy that raced through her body and curled like a storm of its own deep in her cunt?

Did she know how it felt to Kay to let it go?

Shana slipped off her blouse. Kay unhooked her bra, slipped it off, traced her fingers over Shana's brown breast. She curled her hand into a fist for the texture between her curled fingers and ran it over Shana's hardening nipple.

Shana gasped, pulled Kay close, slid painted fingers under Kay's shirt. She curled her long nails over Kay's back just hard enough to make Kay growl. A clap of thunder drowned out the sound.

Kay's shirt hit the floor in a crumpled heap. She looked at Shana looking at her tattoos.

"I can see it on them," Shana whispered. "Like silver."

Kay looked down at herself, the muscles she'd sculpted and the pictures she'd had someone else ink into her skin. Sometimes her body felt wrong, no matter how she built it or adorned it. Sometimes she kept her breasts hidden even here, even with Shana.

But when Shana saw her lightning, curled all around her like a sacred gift, she forgot to be ashamed.

Shana slid her hands away. She reached down to open the zipper of her skirt. Kay waited for her to pull it off, but she only slid her hands away and laughed.

Rain lashed the windows and Shana squirmed. Lightning seared the sky again, just so Kay could watch it brighten Shana's face.

Then Kay yanked Shana's skirt down. Kay spared only a glance for the lace panties Shana was wearing. They might have tantalized her before, but the gathering storm came with a need she couldn't slow, and she yanked them down without a thought.

Kay reached down to slide her hands over Shana's hips. Her hands were paler and blunter than Shana's and the soft skin under her fingertips made her feel strong and proud and awkward all at once.

She slipped one finger between Shana's legs, closed her eyes, and focused on the softness of the skin she found there. Shana was already wet, and when Kay's finger slid up to find her clit, Shana arched and moved into the touch.

Rain lashed against the windows, rattling the glass, and a clap of thunder swallowed Shana's moan.

"Fuck me," Shana whispered. That, Kay heard, under the fierce force of rain and the echoes of the thunder.

She smiled, and lightning lit the sky again. Shana stared up at her and licked her lips.

Kay unzipped her jeans and freed the cock strapped at her hips, eternally as ready and greedy as she felt right now. Shana turned her face away like she meant to be modest, but Kay saw a smirk curl her reddened lips.

She grabbed hold of Shana's legs. Shana looked over at her arms, a sly little look in her eyes. In one sudden burst of movement and strength, Kay pulled her close. Shana gasped again and tilted her hips up to meet her.

Kay wrapped a hand around her cock, closed her eyes again, moved her hand over it. She wasn't supposed to feel anything, not now, not with this, and even a tiny bit of magic wasn't supposed to fix that. But sliding the head of her cock over Shana's waiting lips and seeing the moisture glisten there made her shiver anyway, the lightning speeding through her and crackling forth again just outside the window.

She took a deep breath, opened her eyes, and plunged in.

Shana pushed her legs wider apart. Kay growled, the thunder long and low under her voice, and moved as slow as she could stand. Shana's legs locked around her, strong and possessive.

Lightning lit the sky again and Kay wrapped her hands around Shana's hips and moved faster. Rain crashed against the windows and she drove deeper and deeper and pulled back to push in again. Shana threw back her head and opened her painted mouth and Kay made the lightning flash again, wanting to sear it into her vision, into her memory.

Shana canted her hips again, moving with Kay's thrusts, and when she lifted her head she stared straight into Kay's eyes. She didn't need to imagine the threads of silver and light that Shana would see in her gaze right now because she could feel it all herself, a steady crackling buzz of light and heat that meant it didn't matter where Kay's body ended and Shana's began, if it ever had.

Kay didn't always come like this, despite the heat and the warmth moving through her. It didn't matter, not most of the time, not with Shana's gasps and cries filling her ears and the feeling when her body locked, and trembled, and let go.

But this time, the storm was with her, and this time, the thunder was hers, and when the last bolt of lightning came to claim them it wouldn't matter if it was flesh, or magic.

For them, it had always been both.

And tonight, the lightning followed her.

THE CYBORG HE BROUGHT HOME

"WHAT IS *that* doing here?"

Jake looked up from his mug of bloodroot tea. The tea was good enough, but there wasn't much left in his cup. It wasn't like he was about to do some massive working and needed it to help him focus.

He was just here with Sarah. To talk, to relax, maybe to do some practicing after if the tea helped enough. But he'd probably end up talking to Sarah, honestly. Magic wasn't the kind of thing you could rush along. Or at least, Jake didn't try. Not unless he really needed it.

And right now, Sarah was jabbing a finger toward the door. Lightning crackled over her tattoos, and a tiny flame ignited in her hair.

Jake tensed, his own tattoos beginning to glow. No one interesting came in here, but it helped to be ready, just in case. The magic pulsed in the ink at his palms, ready to become fire like Sarah's hair, or to shift the doorframe into tangling vines, or envelop the table in a protective ward.

But there was nothing in the doorway. Just a crowd of people walking in, most of them covered in tattoos, like Jake and Sarah. A bunch of wizards, coming in to have a drink. Or to choke down a few gulps of traditional tea before practicing their charms and wards.

And I thought something might actually happen, Jake thought. The heat in his hands faded.

Then he saw it.

A flash of red. A gleam like light on metal.

Metal?

He looked over at a pale-skinned, redheaded man, his hair tied into a bun at the back of his head.

His clothes looked unusual. Made of some tight-fitting, tailored mesh that clung to his muscular frame. The light playing on it gave it a satiny sheen. Was that the glimmer Jake had seen? It wasn't red, more a grayish silver.

But the lights in here could do strange things. Especially if some young mage felt like playing tricks.

The stranger looked out of place here in a bar that some old hippie nature mages twisted out of a pair of big trees about a hundred years ago. Maybe he came from one of the colonies in some far-off solar system. Or from a moon, at least.

But that wasn't what caught Jake's eye. He'd seen something red, not gray.

He looked closer at the man's hair. Bright red. And not just bright, but shiny.

Metallic, like he'd thought before.

Illusionists could do that. Make their hair shine like gold. Like a princess in a fairy tale. Make sure their every movement dazzled. But Jake was a wizard. He knew how to spot a glamor. He knew what to look for; he'd see a shimmer, a faint shift of color, a haze around the person weaving the illusion, especially if he were looking for it.

Which meant this man's hair was actually made of metal.

"A cyborg," Jake breathed, and tried not to stare.

He'd seen cyborgs before, but not often. And not here. In Greentree, people stuck to magic.

Most of the time, anyway. Jake glanced around and caught the glow of a phone in someone's hand, and smirked.

Easier than telepathy, and less likely to give you a headache.

Besides, the only people who went in for that "wise old archmage" shit were old men. The kind that dressed in robes, chanted all the time, and made sure their tattoos looked fancy. Leaves and curls and flourishes, like their magic wouldn't work if they stuck to boring black lines.

Jake shook his head. Most of them discovered their magic late anyway. They showed off just to pretend they'd grown up with it. That they hadn't found out they were wizards about six months before they came to Greentree.

Jake saw no need to hide his phone or his yearning for a nice hoverbike, someday when he got far enough away from Greentree to actually buy one. And he liked a good pair of jeans and his old leather jacket much better than robes. They fit him and felt good. Why bother with a damn dress you had to learn how not to trip over?

He winked at the cyborg and took his hand off the handle of his mug. He laid his hand palm-up on the table and conjured a small flame. Nothing fancy. A magician-child's first trick.

But if the cyborg hadn't seen much magic in his life, it might just impress him.

The flames flickered, yellow and green. The tattoos on the back of Jake's hand glowed brighter.

Not everyone here hates you. Also, you're kind of cute.

Telepathy would make the message clearer. But that would hurt Jake's head. And magic fire was more interesting anyway.

He'd always thought cyborgs would be tall. Big guys who towered over all the peons with normal skeletons. But this guy was short, shorter than Jake. Pale-skinned, like Jake had noticed before, with a smattering of freckles. A tuft of bright red beard sprouted from his chin and sparser fuzz roughened his cheeks.

Jake's hands twitched. That would be nice to touch. And seemed ordinary somehow, like any other guy. Jake liked that. He would've worried too much if the cyborg looked too perfect.

But not everything about the newcomer looked human. And Jake liked that even more.

The hair was obvious, fine coppery fibers gleaming in the light. Jake grinned. A cyborg wouldn't need hair, would he? Or if those wires did something—connected him to some network, even out here in the Wilds—would they need to be so fine?

But it wasn't just the hair on his head. Part of the man's forehead shimmered, too. It was the same color as his skin, but without any freckles and, when he moved, Jake could see it had a pearly sheen. Had he been burned or injured? Or did cyborgs just get whole new scalps, skin and hair and all?

A circle of metal surrounded—*replaced?* Jake wondered—one ear, and a thin coil of metal slid from it to the edge of his lip.

Even better than a phone, Jake thought. But for all Jake knew it was a hearing aid instead.

The cyborg looked down at Jake's fire, then up into his face. He didn't say anything, but the corner of his mouth quirked up in a smile. His eyes were hazel. Nothing too special. But they glowed, too, too bright to be natural. Like a mage's eyes when he got really absorbed in deep magic.

Jake thought he saw them iris open like something mechanical. Watching him and studying him. Maybe even zooming in, like a camera.

He smiled and laughed and tried to look enticing.

He was just looking down at the cyborg's hands—pearly like his head and neck—when a huff from Sarah brought him back to himself.

"What?" he said, pretty sure he already knew.

"Don't tell me you're flirting with that thing."

Jake turned his hand over to cover his magical fire. It warmed his hand and died under his palm. He stared at the tattoos on the back of his hand to keep from glaring too hard. The bright green of the magic burned into his vision.

"So what if I am?" he asked, not looking back at her.

"You—"

"That one's not even a man."

Jake's head snapped up. The deep, low rumble wasn't Sarah's voice. And the tone wasn't a gentle reprimand.

He stared up at a big man, broad and burly, his tattoos full of jagged lines and sharp thorn patterns. They covered his bald head and curled down to his cheeks.

Tough guy, Jake thought. The thorns might mean he could make plants grow and catch you in thick or spiky vines. That would be bad, considering almost everything in here was shaped from a tree. But the brown and silver sparks flickering at his fingertips might mean rock and stone instead. The kind of guy who'd make a big show of tossing boulders at you if he didn't like you.

And probably miss. Too easy to get away.

Besides, there weren't any big rocks in the bar. Jake did his best to glare back. "Not a man? Last I checked, cyborgs were people."

"You're a fool." The man's brows knotted, and his eyes glittered with magic.

Jake scowled. Was this guy really going to pick a fight with him just for flirting? His tattoos itched, warm with the fire he'd conjured before.

"He's a man," Jake repeated, more insistent. "That doesn't change just because he's got metal bits."

The light in the man's eyes flickered. "Not the metal bits I'm talking about."

"Not the—" That stopped Jake up short. "Then what the hell are you even—?"

Sarah slid forward and reached a hand between them. Her own eyes flared red, and lightning crackled over a pattern of lines inked on her neck. Her hair glowed, too, incandescent with the first hints of flame.

"You can leave," Sarah said, giving the big man the exact look Jake had been trying for.

I don't need you to defuse this, he thought. Even though Sarah setting him on fire was probably a better plan than— whatever Jake's plan was.

The big mage snorted. "Just thought he might like to know."

He stomped off. Jake watched him go, his hands and wrists glowing.

The fire in Sarah's hair died with a little plume of smoke. "Jake—"

Jake reached out and almost touched Sarah's wrist before he remembered not to singe her. "Don't tell me you agree with that jerk."

She frowned. "Agree with him? He felt like picking on you. Why would I agree with that?"

"You're looking at me like you just looked at him. Also, your eyes are still red."

"We're wizards, Jake. Not machines. Who knows what Baldy knows about him?"

"He doesn't know anything."

Sarah sighed. The fire in her eyes dimmed, but smoke curled up from her hair again. "I still think you're making a mistake."

Jake grinned. This he could handle.

"Then let me make it," he said.

Sarah shook her head. She got up, sighing, and before she even turned away, Jake knew she was going to walk out.

Not that it mattered. Everything would be fine between them tomorrow. Hell, she'd probably want to know all about it. He smiled at her back and turned back to his tea. It had cooled some, but bloodroot tea was never tasty anyway.

"Thank you," a voice said.

Jake looked up to see the cyborg sit down. Right next to him.

Jake's grin widened. The magic brightened his eyes and warmed his temples. But even as the cyborg took his seat, a few chairs scooted further away from them, some by magic, the roots under them twisting up and away with mages still sitting on them.

Jerks.

"No problem." Tattooed lines at Jake's temples flickered

with magic.

A smile spread over the bearded face. "My name's Cory."

Cory rested his hands on the table, and Jake allowed himself to stare. The light played on their surface, like the first hints of magic glittering in someone's ink. And they were sleek. Too smooth, too perfect. Jake wondered what they'd feel like on his skin and shivered.

Jake's own hands were brown. Too mottled and veiny next to Cory's sculpted perfection. Even the ink tracing lines of power over his skin looked crude to him now.

The sheen of his magic dimmed, only a few stray motes of green light winking in them, which made it easy to see the places where the black ink had faded, where the tattooist's lines hadn't been perfectly straight.

It didn't matter here in Greentree where everyone was all Back To Nature anyway. But to a cyborg, with hands and hair shaped to who knew what kinds of exact specifications, with gods knew what enhancing one of his ears?

Cory didn't seem to mind, though. He looked down at the tattoos, and his eyes got big again. His pupils widened, and the irises of his eyes glowed bright like a mind-mage's.

"Magic," Cory said, still looking at Jake's hands.

Yeah, Jake thought. That should have been obvious and boring, but the way Cory said it—

Jake closed his eyes, took a deep breath, and felt heat zip through his ink again. It blossomed from his palms in another flower of green-tinted flame. He opened his eyes and watched Cory watch it.

Someone cleared his throat nearby. Jake bit back a sigh but didn't open his eyes just yet.

"So does the robot want anything," said a voice, "or is he just going to sit there mooning over you?"

"He's not a—" Jake began, but Cory waved one of those perfect hands.

"You're right," Cory said. "I should be ordering something." He looked around at the mages gathered in the bar, those eerie eyes lingering on some of the fancier mugs in front of them. Some were handcrafted, carved with runes and sigils. A few glowed, the drinkers' magic activating the charm.

"But I don't know what to get." He cast a glance at the dregs of bloodroot tea in Jake's mug. "What were you having?"

"Just tea. Traditional drink. Supposed to help you focus on your magic." Jake looked down at the pattern of tattoos on his arms and shook his head.

"Tea is fine," Cory said. "I'm more thirsty than anything else. Is it any good?"

The bartender was frowning. Jake could guess why. Bloodroot tea was a wizard thing.

"I like it. But I've been drinking it since I was an apprentice. Gods know I needed whatever help focusing could find." He looked back at Cory. "You can—I'll buy you something stronger, if you want."

Cory smiled at Jake and looked around again. He looked at the ceiling, the beams woven of living tree wood. He looked at the lamps, magical flames flickering in different colors, first yellow, then warm orange, then bright amber red and back again. This time Jake was close enough to see that his irises did shift, mechanically clicking from one setting to another. Jake looked down at his tattooed arms again, at the dark hair growing on them.

If Cory had enhanced vision, did he like what he saw?

Cory looked at the cup of tea again. "Well, I came here to see how the mages live. I don't have any magic, but I might as well see what it's like."

"I've got it." Jake pulled out his wallet. The ink on his palm flashed green and he levitated some coins, for effect. Cory watched them, suitably awed.

The bartender made a disgusted noise and snatched up the coins before they had a chance to hit the table.

Glowing eyes watched him. When he turned away, Cory reached out and wrapped a hand around Jake's wrist.

Jake braced himself for the cold metal of a lifeless machine. But Cory's hands were warm as skin.

His fingertips were smooth, smooth and polished, like a

water-worn seashell. And over it all was an electrical feeling, like the crackle of a storm in the air. Or like Sarah's lightning, only cooler. Crisper.

The smoothness wrapped around Jake's hand. He let it. Cory turned his hand, palm up, the movement unimaginably gentle.

No conjured flame in the way now. Just the green glow of the magic running through Jake's ink, a glyph of calling traced into his palm years and years ago. The ink had faded a lot—palms did that—but it didn't matter. Not with the magic running through it, making it brilliant and bright.

"Your hand is warm," Cory said, the hint of a laugh in his voice.

"So's yours."

The tea didn't go over well. But then, Cory was the only person who'd expected it to. He drank it, though, his lips curling with every sip. Jake laughed.

Cory grinned back at him over the rim of the cup and set it down, defeated. "Wizards can keep their tea."

"I told you so."

But bad as the tea was, Cory didn't seem to mind it. And Jake was tired of being stared at. And if he wanted back in Sarah's good graces, he'd better have a story to tell her about all this when he saw her again.

"So," he began. "Did you just want to feel a magical tattoo and try bitter beverages no one likes, or were you actually interested?"

Cory laughed. "You're not afraid of me."

"Afraid of you? I've been trying to get your attention since you walked in the door."

"Yeah, I noticed." The sculpted hand curled around the teacup. "So do you always pick up traveling riff-raff from moon colonies or is it just me?"

"Why shouldn't I? My house has more wards than my skin. If you tried anything, they'd either knock you back fifty feet or fry all your electronics."

Or maybe they wouldn't. The old guys who played archmage liked to talk about how wizardry was better than technology, but you couldn't trust a damn word they said.

Not that it mattered. Jake had had been intrigued the moment he'd seen Cory's metallic hair. All this just confirmed how much he wanted Cory to come home with him.

Cory chuckled at Jake's boast. But those machine-eyes ratcheted wide, wider, too wide to be human.

Shit. This tricked-out guy who's half muscle and half metal, and you scare him off talking about a few spells of protection? Fantastic.

"Look, it's okay if you don't—"

"I do. I definitely do." But he looked down at Jake's hand without touching it. Like he didn't want to. Or like he couldn't.

"Then what's the problem? If you think I don't want you just because you're half metal, you haven't been paying attention."

"That's not why I think you might change your mind."

He looked over Cory's muscular frame, stared at the metallic hands. "What did you do, blow up half a moon or something?"

Cory laughed. "Nah." Then he looked away, toward the door the bald man had stormed out of. "That guy—the big one, who came over to talk to you—"

"He was a jerk."

Cory kept looking at the door. "He was warning you about me, wasn't he?"

Jake's tattoos itched. "He wasn't making any sense."

"No. That's the thing. He probably was making sense."

Jake reached out to touch Cory's chin, his hand still hot with magic. Cory's eyes flickered and he flinched, but he didn't pull away.

Good.

"Look at me," Jake said.

Cory did. His eyes even widened again, like he understood it was important.

"Are you interested in me or not?"

Cory's lip quirked into a grin. "Yeah."

Jake let the magic flow through him. "Then tell me on the way."

He leaned closer, drew Cory's chin toward him with magicked fingers.

The hell with damn fools who throw rocks. The hell with Sarah.

He reached out to move the microphone at Cory's lips aside, tried not to think about what that might mean messing up. Then he pressed his lips to Cory's.

They were soft, full, and perfectly human.

Everything about the forest intrigued Cory. Or so it seemed from the sheer number of questions he kept asking Jake.

He wanted to know whether every twist in every tree trunk was natural or magical. Whether every light was electrical, natural, or lit by wizardry. He stopped at each one Jake told him about, reaching out with those metallic hands.

Jake wished Cory would touch him instead. The slow, warm burn of his magic and his lust—all woven together, all parts of him—had felt good at first. Now it was just getting annoying.

And Cory couldn't stop talking about the bar, the way the two trees wound together. Apparently, he thought it was romantic.

Jake thought it was creepy. Who knew what the trees wanted? Too many wizards showing off too much.

He kept looking over at Cory, at the grey mesh of his shirt. It showed off his muscles, and that was nice. But it also made him wonder where Cory came from. Had he said something about a moon, or had Jake been too busy remembering what his hands felt like to pay attention?

Either way, the silvery fabric made Jake think of stars. And not the ones the High Mages stared at when they could look up through the trees or levitate over them. Not the ones that supposedly dictated your destiny and influenced your magic. The ones sleek spaceships visited, and chrome-shiny colonies orbited.

"You had something you wanted to tell me?" Jake said at last.

Cory stared ahead. "Yeah. I did."

But he didn't say anything. Just stood there and stared.

Jake sighed. "Look. Telepathy gives me a headache. I'm not gonna be reading your mind."

Cory laughed.

"You're the one who wanted me to know something. If you want me to know it, you're gonna have to tell me."

"I—the modifications you see aren't my only ones."

Jake smirked. "Are you telling me that when I get you home, what I find will surprise me?"

A smile spread over the bearded face. "Something like that."

"And you think cybernetic parts I can't see right now are going to make me want you less?"

Cory shook his head. The smile was gone. "That guy. In the bar. What was it he said about me?"

"That he didn't like your mods."

Except that wasn't it at all, was it?

Cory's head snapped up with a tiny mechanical click. Jake watched his irises widen, looking for the lie.

"That you're not—that you're not really a man," Jake tried.

Cory nodded, his face grave. "That's what I thought."

"You know the guy? He's a wizard. He's one of us."

"I don't know him well. But we've crossed paths." Cory chuckled, a dry mirthless laugh. "I'd never have thought of wandering off to some forest full of wizards if I'd never met one."

"You're here because of that jerk?"

"No. I'm here because I wanted to meet some mages who weren't jerks."

And you came here? Jake laughed, still nervous. "But—he said you're not a man."

"Some people would say that."

Jake looked at him. The hair, the beard, the muscular

body he couldn't see yet but had spent the past hour guessing about. "Why?"

"Some people would say I used to be a woman."

Jake stopped walking. His tattoos flared, a bright flicker of surprise. "You're—?"

Cory nodded. "Some people would say no matter what I change, I still am."

Jake stared ahead like the trees really had secrets. And like they could actually tell him some of them, the way the old men liked to pretend. He'd heard of people like—like Cory, apparently. But he only knew one.

They'd called him—*her*, Jake reminded himself. *She* was a *her* now. If she'd ever been anything else.

Anyway, they'd called her Greentree's mermaid. A mind-mage and illusionist who wove such thick glamors around herself she floated in a halo of iridescence.

Even the few people in Greentree who didn't have magic could see it. But it didn't matter. She was going for illusion, and everybody knew it.

She didn't just use her mind-magic to make people see a big bust and thick, round hips. When she performed, she played the part of a siren. Complete with illusions of gills at her throat, webbed fins for ears, and scales that matched her dark brown skin. Her braided hair faded into a spray of sea foam, and with a few little mind tricks, the light on her sequined dresses moved like gentle waves.

Jake could never tell if she had a good voice, or if that was more glamor. Magic, slinking its way into your ears until her song echoed through your head, low and haunting. Was that what made men want her, too? The siren's song?

Jake didn't know. He'd never been a fan of illusionists and had never been interested in women. Or drag queens, like he'd thought she was. But queen or woman, she'd always been one of the best mind-mages Greentree had. Everybody knew that, too.

It didn't mean they liked how she used her magic, though. They'd whispered, a lot. *Why use gifts like that for some cheap magicked-drag act?*

Still, they tolerated her. You didn't just slam doors on talent like that, no matter what someone chose to do with it.

But then she'd left, and the whispers had just gotten louder. Magic was natural. Hormones weren't.

Illusions were just magic. A pretty popular kind of magic, too. Any telepath or trickster knew a few of them and probably more. If you were good at them, okay, making yourself look like a mermaid was fine. Frivolous, maybe, when you were supposed to be Calling Up the Deep Magic or whatever. But fine.

So was making yourself look like a woman. If that was something you really wanted to do.

But changing yourself into one wasn't.

Jake never liked that. He had no love for illusionists. Anyone who could play mind games without a splitting migraine to show for it was dangerous. But he'd never liked their whispers, like one of their best mind-mages wasn't worth missing.

And now—

"You're—?" Jake squinted at Cory and hoped he didn't look angry.

Cory blushed and shook his head. "I was a scrappy little asshole. You kind of have to be an asshole if you're living on a moon."

"I imagine you would," Jake said. Like he knew something about living on moons.

"Nobody looks out for you. People pick fights." The metallic hands tightened into fists, compact and sleek. How bad would it hurt if one of those punched you in the face or in the gut? Jake shuddered. Even magic wouldn't help you much with that.

"Everybody decent runs off to a planet as soon as they can," Cory went on. He looked around at the trees again. Up at the light coming through them.

It really was pretty. Jake wondered when he'd stopped noticing. He was supposed to be a nature mage. How had he stopped looking up?

"Well, I figured I'd be a bigger asshole. Cover for my size."

Jake laughed. *Yeah, I was already figuring you could punch someone's lights out, short or not.*

"I wasn't happy. I didn't know why. I got into fights all the time. Picked fights when they didn't find me. That's stupid as hell, on a moon."

"But your mods—I mean, the metal ones."

"Yeah. Got the eyes so I could see better, the hands so I could punch."

The pearled fists unfolded, opening. "I liked it. Knowing I could change. I didn't like the body I had. I felt more real. Less... itchy in my skin. So I kept going."

He smiled. "And here I am."

Jake looked him over again. He'd noticed Cory was small for a guy but not much else. Was—was he supposed to notice things? His voice, his face, his shape? Or was that just rude?

The kind of rude that gets you punched, Jake thought. He'd told Cory he wanted this, even when he knew Cory had a Big Secret. Now what was he doing?

Stick to wondering what other mods he's got, Jake told himself.

He hoped he could follow his own advice. He couldn't stop staring at Cory, wondering about things he knew he shouldn't.

"So if you wanted to know whether I want to go with you, yes. Yes. Of course I do. Are you sure you want me to come with you?"

Jake closed his eyes and took a deep breath, in and out. Like boring instructors taught you to meditate before deep magic. You were supposed to visualize, too. But visualize what? Cory? Himself with Cory? The body he'd expected Cory to have? The body he might have now?

What did he really want?

He thought of Cory's hands, the pearly-smooth metal. Of the power in them, frightening and promising all at once. Of their touch, strange and welcoming. He'd liked that. He'd wanted more of that.

Was he really going to let that go, just because he didn't know what to expect?

He took another breath. Shaky. Uneven. Not like the meditator he was trying to be. He wanted to be like himself. Like Jake.

He opened his eyes.

"Yeah."

Rich mages sculpted their homes from wood, like the bar in Greentree, shaping living trees to their will and carving wards and sigils into the bark. Jake wasn't rich.

And nobody had time to do all of that tree-shaping anyway except the old men who'd never admit they did it because they were bored.

But he did have sigils everywhere, painted on the walls, carved into the wood. Some of it was just old graffiti, vulgar little messages left by kids who needed the protection. They might hex you if you triggered them, maybe. But most were so old they'd been used up long ago.

Jake hadn't minded. Every little bit helped. And the risk of triggering some weak little curse from a century ago kept life exciting anyway.

Also, it meant he could add his own glyphs and wards without too many people noticing and worrying about them, one of the perks of being easily distracted and being a doodler if you had magic to go with it.

He pressed his hand to the door. The wood was old and scratchy-splintery, and sometimes he liked that and sometimes he hated it.

At his touch, it warmed. The wood under his hand glowed white, and the magic raced outward, tracing the shape of the biggest glyph traced onto it. The glyph flared once and faded, little glittering motes of light still flickering. With a creak, the door slid open.

"All that for a lock?" said Cory. He reached out a sculpted hand and touched the surface of the door. His eyes narrowed to slits, glowing like a wizard's.

The simplest stuff impresses you, thought Jake. *I could get used to this.*

"A lock and a ward, like I told you."

"Keeping the riff-raff out? Maybe it doesn't work as well as you thought."

Jake ignored him. "None of the shmucks who were giving you the evil eye in the bar can get near this house right now. You're safe. As long as you stop gawking at the door and come inside."

Cory glared at him but walked obediently into the room. The magic shut the door behind him.

Jake watched his legs move. It looked natural enough, but purposeful. Like his legs were built for movement and that's what they did. No slouching or shuffling. Like his fist, and the way it fit together, too.

"Worried for me?" Cory said.

Jake snickered. "These are the Wilds. You never know."

"No. I don't guess I do."

"But you get along fine on moons. Don't act too innocent."

"All right then." Cory stepped closer. He slid aside the microphone at his lip. "I won't."

A metal-smooth hand wrapped around the back of Jake's head. Jake's temple-tattoos flared green in anticipation. Fingers twined themselves in his long hair and pulled his head down.

Jake looked back at Cory. The machine-eyes widened, too wide. They glowed.

Then Cory kissed him, hard. Jake gave into it, closing his eyes and opening his mouth. His cock stirred, and the tattooed skin of his pelvis tingled, his magic as eager as the rest of him.

He moaned and wrapped his hands around Cory's back. His fingertips skipped over the mesh, not sure if there was flesh or metal under the fabric, wanting to know and not caring all at once.

Jake broke the kiss, panting. Half from desire and half

because he wanted Cory to know that *yes, he wanted this; yes, he liked this; no, it didn't matter what he was expecting because this wasn't about what he expected at all.*

He rubbed his cheeks against the bristly fuzz on Cory's cheeks. "That's—"

"Real?" Cory finished for him and laughed.

Dammit. "I didn't mean—"

"I grew it myself, if that's what you wanted to know."

Jake grinned against Cory's cheek. "All right."

He slipped off his jacket and let it fall. Usually he hung it over something—everybody had to have some little thing they loved and took care of, even Jake—but Cory was sliding his fingers under Jake's shirt.

Jake let out a ragged, heavy breath. The tattoos on his chest began to warm and glow, his magic responding to the touch of polished fingers. And over it all, the electrical, ozone crackle Jake had felt before. His magic pulsed in answer to it, a bright flare of light.

"Did I—is my hand hurting you?"

"No."

"Then let's see you," he said, and pulled off Jake's shirt.

Jake stared down at himself. By now, the patterns were so intimately familiar he barely noticed them anymore.

"Pretty," Cory said. "What do they mean?"

His finger moved over a spiral of curved points that radiated outward from the middle of Jake's chest. Little sparks rose where his fingers passed. Jake felt the little shocks, like Sarah's lightning, almost, only better. Different. Special. Something he would only feel once.

"Out from the heart," Jake made himself say. "The source. Brings it out."

Cory nodded. His hand slid over the zigzag of light and moved up toward Jake's shoulders. His fingertips slid along Jake's shoulder and down his arm.

"To your hands."

"Yes."

"And this?"

His other hand reached down to Jake's abdomen. Ink covered his belly, all circle and sphere. Thorns curved out from its, center warning anyone who wished him harm. The pattern faded into diagonal lines at his sides, all energy and movement.

"It's for safety," Jake admitted. He put his hands on his hips. "Bad guys: fuck off."

"Another ward?"

"Yeah."

Cory smirked. "I like that. Means I'm safe with you."

Jake grinned back. "Oh, is that what you think?"

"Maybe not." The metal traced a line leading out from the ward, down toward Jake's groin.

"And this?"

Jake's hand caught Cory's wrist before he could reach for it. "Let's see you first."

A shadow of a frown curled Cory's fuzzed lip. He looked down. Jake saw light shimmer in his metallic hair.

"Don't worry," Jake said. The light coursing through his ward brightened. *You can't be more nervous than me right now.*

"All right," Cory said, and he looked up again. The metal hands reached for zippers on the sides of his shirt and undid them.

The chest beneath was pale and muscular, covered with a smattering of red hair. Just under his pecs ran the pale pink lines of two long-healed scars.

Jake reached out and ran his fingers over them. Next to the bright eyes, the shining hair, the iridescent, sculpted arms, a scar seemed somehow wrong. Rough. Vulnerable. "These are—"

"I had breasts, Jake."

Jake winced. Was that an explanation or a *Dammit, do I have to explain everything to this guy?*

"Right, but I mean—you're already half metal. You could look like whatever you want."

"That's true, I could."

"So why keep a scar?"

"Because they're mine, Jake. They remind me of where I've been and what it took to get to where I am now." Cory put his hand over Jake's. "I'm not a robot. Whatever the people outside might say."

"No." Jake tried to smile. What could he say to that? "No, you're not."

Well, if I can't find words, there's always my magic.

He closed his eyes, drew it from its core inside him. A bright heat, in his mind, in his gut, at his heart. The tattoos along his arms tingled, expectant. Then it coursed down them, following the lines of his body, down to his fingertips, a crackle of heat under his fingerprints.

He traced the scars again by feel alone. Cory's breath hitched, and he made a strangled little sound.

"Magic," he said, like he'd said before, with the same catch in his voice.

Jake grinned. *I really could get used to this.*

"Says the guy with perfect arms. Made out of who-knows-what."

Jake took a long look at them. The metal reached past Cory's shoulders, shimmered at his collarbones. It matched his hands, creamy white to match his pale skin, but with the same pearled sheen as his fingers, wrists, and palms.

Jake kept staring. Cory lifted them, flexed, extended them, let the light play over them. His lips curled in a grin. Apparently Jake wasn't the only one who liked showing off.

Cory's arms were broad and strong. Big, like someone who'd built up muscle through hard work, but the metal segments curled and curved in shapes too fluid to quite match a human shape. Jake stared at the seams, wondering what it would feel like to touch them.

So he did, running his fingertips over a groove between Cory's tricep and bicep. Cory narrowed his eyes and made a low little sound.

"Wait," said Jake, catching sight of a patch of exposed skin and muscle on one arm. He reached out to touch that too. "This bit isn't metal."

"Skin and muscle," Cory said. "That's where my implant is."

"Implant?"

Cory flexed his arm. "Hormones. How I grew this beard you like so much. Why my voice is deep."

Oh. "Yeah. I should have guessed."

He moved a hand to Cory's bearded chin, his fingertips still aglow. He remembered the man in the bar, his disgust and anger. At the metal. At what he knew, or thought he knew, about Cory.

We're wizards, he thought. *Go too far out of Greentree and it's us they're talking about.*

"So," said Cory.

Jake looked up. "So."

"So you wanted to see me before you'd let me see you. So what do you think?"

"I think it's—they're—" Jake swallowed. *Words.*

If he hadn't been hard before, he was hard now. Maybe that would be enough? But Cory was still staring at him, eyes alien and eager, and waiting for him to say *something.*

"I think *you're* beautiful. If that's how I'm supposed to say it. I mean, if that doesn't sound too much like—"

Cory chuckled. "I'll take it." He tilted his coppery head toward the bedroom door. "Let's go inside."

Like everything else, Jake's bed was a mess. He usually didn't notice until he had to change the sheets, and he didn't worry about anyone else caring either. Not usually. But now he glared at the rumpled covers like he expected the thing to make itself.

He could fix it right now with his magic if he really wanted to. But they'd already walked inside and magicking it up pretty would just make the mess he'd started with more obvious.

Cory didn't seem to mind. He pulled his shoes and socks off, offering Jake a tantalizing glimpse of shimmering feet that might or might not have actual toes. Then he pulled the balled-up covers back and laid down like he belonged there.

He smirked up at Jake. "It's your turn now."

Are you still nervous? Jake thought. But all he said was "So it is," and stripped off his jeans.

Too fast, probably. An illusionist would have made this a show. Especially with all this looking at each other. But Jake wasn't the type to play games. He gave Cory a moment to stare at the outline of his cock through his briefs and then pulled them down.

Lines of ink ran from his ward to his pelvis, then traced their way up his length. A small design adorned the head—a pattern meant to represent a waking eye. But he was too hard right now, looking at Cory looking at him, for Cory to see that.

"That's impressive." Cory's eyes flickered with light. Was that a natural response, or was Cory doing it on purpose to tease him? Was that how you smirked or winked when you had enhanced eyes?

How many gestures did they have like that, on faraway moon colonies where everyone had metal bits? How much had he missed, just talking to Cory today?

Stick to what you know, he thought.

"Magic runs through everything," he said. He let the energy speed through him, felt it flicker through his already-sensitive flesh. "Head, heart, hands, belly. Why would it stop there?"

Cory said something, but Jake didn't hear it. He closed his eyes at the flicker of sensation. It felt almost like fingers moving over him, and all he could think was how much he wanted Cory's quicksilver hands on him.

He stepped closer.

Cory grinned. "So that glows if I touch it, too. Right?"

He reached out and wrapped a hand around Jake's shaft, his palm all silky-sleek warmth. Little pinpricks of sensation came with the movement, a faint scintilla of static. It didn't sting, only flickered over him, pricking his nerves awake.

Obediently, his magic flared. He opened his eyes and

looked at himself, knowing Cory was looking at him. A bright green glow surrounded Cory's hand, peeking through his metal fingertips, making them shimmer with light.

He'd liked the way he looked in someone else's hand since he first got the tattoos. But this—

"Nice trick," Cory was saying, a hint of a laugh in his voice.

It kept Jake from floating away.

"You first," he whispered, and looked up again. "Don't— don't finish this without—"

"So you do want me," Cory said, smiling.

"I do," Jake said. *Whatever you've got.*

Those impossible, shimmering hands pulled away. Jake blinked at the loss, but it didn't really matter. Cory could touch him later. Right now he had to see, had to know—

Cory reached down to undo zippers at the sides of his pants. He peeled them off, revealing matching gray underwear as tight as Jake's, with a bulge in them.

"So you do have—"

"It's metal, too. Is that a problem for you?"

"No," Jake whispered. Which wasn't really necessary. Not from the way his cock had jumped to hear it.

"I didn't think so," Cory said, and slipped his underwear off.

Cory's pelvis shone, wrapped in metal, smooth and segmented. It curved up the sides of his hips and faded at his inner thighs. Like the rest of him, the pieces fit together with sleek seams, some that matched regular human anatomy, some that made new, fluid shapes. Light played off it all, a kaleidoscope of colors laid over metal painted to match flesh.

"I—" Jake said, not even sure what he meant to say.

In the center of the metal, Cory's cock gleamed, iridescent like the rest of him. The metal looked slick, like the hands that had touched him. Like Cory's arms, the shaft had segments, thin seams between one plate and the next.

That must have let it flex, because Cory was just as hard as he was.

"Do you—that's not like—?"

Cory stood up, offering a good look.

But his words were less formal than his pose. "It's my dick. I assume you know how they work."

"Is that some kind of a setting, or—?"

The bearded face flashed him a grin. "What nature gave me's underneath it. It's wired into nerves I already have."

Okay, Jake couldn't quite guess how that worked. But knowing Cory wanted him for real, and not just the metal, but the flesh underneath—

"Then you don't just toggle something? 'I'm ready to play now?'"

"No. That's a natural response." His eyes widened again, and the sudden flicker of light in them must have been mischief. "That's all me."

And you thought I was fancy, Jake thought. "Then you'll feel everything?"

Cory quirked a red eyebrow. "Why don't you find out for yourself?"

Jake didn't need to be asked twice. He dropped to his knees in front of Cory and wrapped his hand around warm metal.

Electricity crackled against the tattoo on his palm, pricking his magic awake. He felt it, too, his heat over Cory's. Was that body heat, warming Cory's metal like it warmed his flesh and skin, or something in the metal?

He opened his mouth and leaned forward to lick. His nose filled with the smell of chrome and ozone, and static crackled on his tongue.

There was no moisture, no slow leak of fluid. But Jake felt the metal twitch, half natural motion and half smooth vibration. The seams between the segments felt strange but good, a ripple of texture as he moved. He murmured in response, his magic a bright surge in skin Cory wasn't even touching any more.

Fingers wound themselves in his hair again. Energy zipped through the tattooed lines at his neck and temple and pooled in a dark spot of ink at his throat.

He wrapped his lips around the head—warm and smooth—and breathed in the sharp, unfamiliar ozone smell. Then he opened his mouth to take Cory in.

Cory's answer was a ragged groan. The altered hands wrapped around Jake's head tightened their grip. It didn't hurt, but Jake could feel the strength in them, alien and superhuman. He moaned around Cory's length.

Cory chuckled. The inexorable hands slid his head up and back down, up and back down, not needing any help from him. He whimpered and opened a throat glittering with magic when he felt something harder and more unyielding than flesh fill it.

I want you to fuck me, Jake thought, squeezing his eyes shut and calling all the power he could draw.

Cory laughed and loosened his grip.

Jake pulled himself off Cory's cock and felt the beginning pulse of a post-telepathy headache thud through his temples. For the first time in his life, he couldn't have cared less.

He lay down on the still-rumpled bed. Cory leaned down and covered Jake's body with his. He pressed the slick warmth of his metallic pelvis to Jake's flesh and moved against him, his movement the smooth slide of something more than human.

Jake panted, too far gone to be embarrassed, and ground back against Cory. The magic surged through his skin at the feel of Cory's cock against him, and a yellow flare of light danced in his vision.

"Please," he said. "If you keep doing this—"

Cory laughed, nodded, and pulled away again.

"The lube is over on that shelf," Jake breathed, pointing. But when he looked up, Cory was already holding up a packet of it. Enhanced reflexes? Or were there cyborg super pockets in his armpits or something?

He watched Cory open the packet and spread the gel over his dick, metal sliding over metal. The gleam of light on the metal and the slow rhythm of the movement mesmerized him.

His hands itched to touch Cory and the tattoos on his

palms burned, bright with the beginnings of flame. But doing that would mean not watching this, and that would be its own loss, too.

He slid down to the edge of the bed and spread his legs wide and kept staring. Only when Cory pressed the head of his cock, sleek and polished like the rest of him, against the rim of Jake's hole did he let himself close his eyes. His magic curled around it, sharp and bright and welcoming.

Cory waited, letting him savor the moment, and then pushed his way inside.

His cock glided into Jake, smooth and unyielding as a piston, pushing him open with a fierce self-assurance Jake had never known before.

The texture was different, too, ribbed from the segments that made up the shaft. Just strange enough to be new, just familiar enough to be right. Jake spread his legs wider and bucked his hips, more eager than he'd ever remembered.

"Easy there," said a voice above him. He saw a flicker of neon light from bright, wide-open eyes. Metallic hands locked around his hips, and his magic was a jagged burst of heat that felt almost as good as Cory moving inside him.

"Please," he said again.

Whether or not Cory heard him, he drove in again and again and again, the friction like a crackling static, and whether that was magic or electricity or just his own desire, Jake neither knew nor cared.

He looked up at the twinkle of eyes and the gleam of copper hair. His hand, ink burning bright as flame, hovered just over his own magic-brightened flesh.

Cory nodded. "I want to see you," he said, his voice a ragged string of breaths.

That was all Jake needed. He wrapped his hand around his own length, magic on magic. It flared through his ink again and he saw its afterimage in the corners of his eyes, a wisp of light. He remembered Cory touching him and whispering, and somehow he knew why Cory might feel awe.

But Cory wasn't here to stare at him, and he wanted more

than that himself. Cory drew back, almost pulling out of him, and slid in again, slow.

"More," Jake gasped, and moved over himself.

Cory growled, low and shapeless, and thrust in again, hard. Jake narrowed his eyes to slits, lost in a world of metal and iridescence, and rocked his hips again, blind.

"I—"

He didn't know if his own mouth or Cory's had made the sound. He heard ragged breaths. An ozone crackle zipped through him. Metal fingers squeezed his hips, almost too tight to bear. He wondered if it would leave him bruised, and flashed his robot man a lopsided smile.

Cory drove him into him again, once, twice, the metal of his palms vibrating in a shudder. Jake worked himself faster, drew a long, low moan from his own throat.

Cory stilled inside him for a moment, panted something that might have been his name, and drew back. Not the slow, even glide of a machine, but the ragged movement of a man, half-gone already and barely able to hold himself back.

So don't, Jake thought, and didn't even know if he'd projected it.

Cory pushed in again, deep and desperate. The metal froze inside Jake again, silent and still, and it felt so familiar that Jake half-expected to feel Cory flood him.

Well, he could do *that* part himself. And felt it starting already, despite that his hand had stilled.

First came a pulse of magic, bright and hot, hot enough to sear his palm. Then his flesh followed, and he shuddered in release, spattering the ink glowing green on his belly.

The lights at the corners of his eyes blossomed in his vision, his magic drowning everything in yellow-white light.

Jake blinked to clear the last motes of light out of his vision. A man half made of metal was staring down at him. He gleamed. "Hi," Jake murmured through a warm haze of satiation.

"Hello." A red-bearded mouth smirked.

Jake propped himself up on his arms. The glow in his ink was already fading. "That was great."

"It was." The metal man sat down next to him. Now that they'd finished, somehow all this seemed unreal. *The Cyborg I Brought Home. Yeah.*

"I should try wizards more often," Cory said, and laughed.

Jake put his hands on his hips. A green gleam lit his eyes. "Wizards. Any wizards? Now that you've slept with this one, you're going to go find another?"

A metallic hand curled around Jake's chin. He let it.

Cory's eyes flickered. Jake hoped it meant mischief. "Is that a problem? We just met."

"No. But maybe I don't want you to leave just yet," Jake said, and leaned in to kiss him again.

BEGINNINGS

THE FINISHERS were lonely.

They shouldn't have been. The outer reaches of space were empty, but they were the Finishers' home. It was proper: silence and solemnity for a being that ended worlds.

If they didn't like the silence, they had their memories. Rock and stone crumbling where they passed. Buildings, built by every hand or claw or prehensile appendage in every galaxy, torn asunder to make way for them. And the cries of the dying, roars or chirps or desperate mumbling, from sapient beings and beasts alike.

The screams were a song, and they carried it with them wherever they wandered among the stars. They had only to think of it, and it would fill their minds, flow from one to the next with no effort and no error.

And if that wasn't enough, the Finishers could mimic the song. They had a thousand mouths, a thousand throats, a thousand lips and beaks and snouts and voice boxes. Borrowing the shape of a mortal creature was as easy as thought—and they shared those already.

And if even that didn't ease their discomfort, they had

each other. A vast web of minds, all linked one to another, all with eons full of memories. They knew one another's thoughts like they knew their own, little lightning shocks of awareness crackling from one to the other, to the other, to the other.

And yet. Discontent flickered through their connection, an anxious thrill. It pricked at their minds, a sharp little sting.

They tried to drown it out, mouths twisting from their surface, shaping themselves into throats and tongues and teeth of every kind. They screamed, over and over, in thousands of voices, the curses and pleas of sapient creatures and the screeches of every kind of beast.

But those cries were only memories, and it had been eons since they had ended a world. It would be almost as long until they were called again.

And even then, the mortals they met would die soon after they arrived.

The thread of worry vibrated fast and bright.

Ending life was their purpose, yes.

But their purpose wouldn't ease their troubles. Not when the problem was the silence.

Not when they needed someone else to fill it.

Vana was lost.

Out beyond the Third Frontier, lost was a bad thing to be.

She'd managed to evade the Legion. Even managed to hide for a few days without being found. But apparently when you were far enough away for those bastards to stop following you, you were too far out for your ship's navigation to know where you were either.

And her ship might run out of fuel any day now.

Vana tightened her hands into fists and spat an array of curses. The ship's computer didn't seem impressed. Vana closed her eyes and forced herself to take a shaky breath in. *Whatever happens now, panic isn't going to help.*

She let her breath out again, heavily, and unclenched her hands. She had some food. Some fuel. Less than she'd like. It had taken her a while to get out here. But she had enough to last her long enough to figure out what to do, as long as she didn't panic.

She paced, for something to do, and squinted at the map again.

It didn't help. The array of stars looked as foreign to her as it did to the computer. She could see planets circling some of them, even a few systems, but...

Can any of those planets support life?

She blinked. "That's it!" she yelled to no one in particular. "Navigation, do any of the three closest systems show signs of organic life?"

It wouldn't get her back to the mothership. It wouldn't connect her to any other Defiers stranded out here, either. Docking with some other unit's ship might look bad, but it wouldn't be the end of the world, no matter what her racing mind might tell her. Joining the Defiers meant knowing things might go wrong.

Finding life out here wouldn't find them. And it wouldn't get her home. But it might keep her from starving while she figured out where the hell she was.

"Life signs detected," the system chirped.

"Yes!" she cried, bouncing. She might blunder into something, but nothing could be as bad as the war back home.

She hoped, anyway.

But when she looked at the readout, something was wrong. It looked almost like the readings she'd get from a planet in the middle of nowhere. A few billion complex life forms, over a large enough space. Except the "planet" didn't seem to be orbiting anything.

"That's weird," Vana muttered. Maybe this wasn't such a good idea, after all. How were you supposed to live on a planet that wandered around the middle of nowhere? Didn't you need heat and light from a sun?

Except apparently a few billion critters had figured that one out. And all Vana had figured out was how to float around like an idiot and wait for her fuel to run out. Or for the Legion to find her. Or for the gods only knew what else.

"Uh, Navigation?"

It didn't answer, of course.

"Set a course for that weird planet full of life signs. And please don't say I told you so if everything goes wrong."

The thing wasn't a planet.

It looked like one at first, big and round. But the colors on its surface had no patterns Vana could see, no mountains or craters or seas. When she got close enough to orbit, some of the random shapes and colors looked too much like faces. Vana guessed that was coincidence, but it still made her hands tighten into fists and her breathing get too fast.

"What are you?" boomed a chorus of voices, making the walls of Vana's ship vibrate.

The planet is yelling at me. Vana opened a hailing frequency, not sure what else to do. "I'm Vana. A human. From Earth."

"No more noise!" the thing answered, a mix of roars and howls and hisses.

Vana swallowed hard. She knew how not to panic until after the Legion ships were gone, but this? Her throat tightened, and she forced herself to breathe. *I have to answer the terrifying alien.* "Noise?"

"From your container. Your metal."

My ship? What did it want her to do, cut the engines?

But before she could bother to ask, the image on her viewscreen grew.

She'd been right about the faces.

Whatever the alien was, it apparently could change its size. It stretched and twisted, glowing as membranes stretched and skin rearranged. Vana saw eyes, glassy and glittering, beady and black. As she watched, the pupils shrank. Irises grew to ring around them. Cat eyes blinked at Vana, then stretched to become something almost human, then split like an insect's compound eye.

Mouths opened and closed, filled with teeth and tongues

and membranes. They made sounds; the ship's speakers reverberated with low groans and echoed with chittering shrieks.

"Hi," Vana whispered, anxiety drying out her mouth. She didn't close her eyes, though. The little part of her the panic didn't own wanted to see this.

The thing wasn't *a* thing. It was... things, plural, all woven together, hands and arms and wings and claws and tentacles winding over and over each other. Scales and fur and skin and feathers, and the oozy gelatin of even weirder creatures. And thousands upon thousands of ears and mouths and eyes.

A whole planet's worth of life forms, all at once.

"No noise," it said. And hissed. And gurgled. One of its faces shifted, a pointed beak smoothing out into a nose and mouth and sprouting lips. Its beady eyes became less round. Eyelids formed around them, and the whites of the eyes began to show. Brows wove over them, hair curling and twisting into a familiar shape.

Vana wasn't sure if that was better or worse.

Her hand hovered over the communication controls. *If you don't want me to make any noise, how am I supposed to keep talking?*

Metal, the thing had said. It didn't like Vana's metal.

The ship?

The communications link?

Is that metal? Do you think we're talking through metal?

"But I'm tiny compared to you," Vana muttered, even as she cut the connection.

Well. Now that she'd done that, she'd have to see if the thing could still hear her. Probably not, but at least that would show it that she wasn't trying to annoy it.

"You're trying to look human," she said, her voice small in her own ears. "You're trying to look like me."

The creature smiled, a bit too wide. Vana felt something— a little pinch inside her head, like the beginning of a headache or the strain from thinking hard—and then the face changed again. Brown skin like Vana's lightened to pale pink and then darkened to rich brown. Eyes widened, shrank, shifted from round shapes to almond, shifted in a spectrum from brown to blue to an unsettling, too-vivid green.

Its features shifted too. The thin lips thickened, full and soft and almost human enough to send thrill through Vana. But then they coarsened, and hair sprouted around them. Vana had never liked men, not like she liked women. Watching this creature try its best to turn into a man only made things weirder.

Vana tried not to look unnerved. "You can hear me."

"We can hear you."

An appendage curled out from the creature—*creatures*, Vana thought. *There's more than one of them. They said "we."*

The limb reaching for Vana's ship looked almost like an arm, a five-fingered brown hand at the end of it, complete with massive fingernails the size of rooms. But it curled and twisted like a worm or a snake, winding itself around Vana's ship.

She heard the crunch of metal and drew in a breath. Her throat tightened, and she couldn't let her breath back out again. The walls dented and warped. They glowed, rings of red and orange and white. Was that hand melting the metal?

Vana wanted to scream, to yell at the alien to stop, to tell it to turn back into a woman while she was at it. But panic constricted her throat, and she gasped out a thin little noise instead. Some dim part of her mind knew that she must have drawn another breath by now, that somehow, she must still have oxygen. But the panic choked her anyway, relentless as always.

I've gotta see this, she told it before it could swallow her bravado in another wave of nerves. *And if this is really happening, I'm dead anyway. So you win. So leave me the hell alone.*

That didn't stop her heart from racing.

The fingers, brown like Vana's and impossibly large, burst through the wall, leaving molten rings of metal where they passed. They moved, blind, and curled over Vana like they meant to pick her up.

Words. She had to say words. She wasn't sure she would be able to gasp them out, not now, not with her head swimming so much she could barely grasp the things going on around her. But she had to try, had to let these aliens know she was human and humans needed air—

"You need not speak."

That was a relief. Too many people didn't just let her panic.

Wait. That was a relief?

Vana you still need to breathe and they're crushing the ship and how the hell are you supposed to explain what oxygen is for?

"Life support," she made herself say. "Status of systems."

"We will provide."

The hand closed around Vana, a wide cage of fingers. They shimmered, lit from within. Was that what their skin looked like, or were they trying to give Vana some light?

And if they could give her light, did that mean they could give her air, too? Was that what they meant by *"we will provide?"*

She could see the space between their fingers, much too big to be airtight. She swallowed hard past the lump in her throat and stepped toward one of the fingers. These creatures didn't want to hurt her, whatever else they were looking for. The least she could do was think, try to make sure they didn't kill her by accident because they didn't quite understand humans.

Wait.

If she was walking, she'd been here a while. Talking to them, thinking at them, walking around on their almost-human palm.

If she had no air, she couldn't have done all that.

"What are you?" she whispered. She reached out to touch the rough, grooved surface of the finger before she could think herself out of it.

The skin in front of her cracked and curled back on itself. Teeth grew to fill the gap, about the size and shape of Vana's own. The skin around them puffed out and became lips, dusky pink and full.

Female this time. As weird as it was to watch a piece of skin turn inside out and grow teeth, Vana appreciated the gesture.

The mouth didn't answer her question. It breathed, slow and easy, in and out.

That was creepy too. Or should've been. Vana grinned wider. "You're getting it."

The mouth exhaled, a warm little gust of wind. Vana breathed it in, surprised enough to let herself breathe deep. The air in her lungs felt good, rich and rejuvenating. *You really are trying.* She stepped closer, the mouth almost even with her own, and breathed deep again.

She felt the little tug in her head again, familiar by now, like being touched on the arm.

That drew her out of whatever strange meditation the aliens had drawn her into. She put her hands on her hips, trying not to feel silly. She'd faced down Legion captains without drowning in her panic. She could do that here. "You didn't answer my question."

Their lip curled in a funny little way. Vana couldn't tell whether it was a smirk or a smile.

"Oh, come on. You don't get to poke around in my head uninvited and not even tell me your names."

"We are the Finishers."

"Finishers, huh? Is that a species?"

"We are the Finishers."

Their voice was beautiful. Distracting, but beautiful. A woman's voice, rich and resonant. And it echoed, like before. Like the woman taking shape was the one talking, but hundreds of other, softer voices were whispering agreement.

"Sure." Vana chuckled. "And I'm a human, and you're a lot bigger than I am, and there's a lot more of you than me. Also, you wrecked my ship and I have no idea how to get back home. So why don't you assume I don't know what you mean and explain to the dumb human what the hell is going on?"

This time, the mouth was definitely laughing. They grew

eyes, just above it, big and brown and almond shaped with little shimmery flecks in the iris. They might have been pretty, if the Finishers hadn't forgotten they needed a nose. But they must have realized their mistake, because one followed, slim and long. Cheeks and forehead followed, sharp and angled. The face pulled free of the skin surrounding it, and hair curled all around it, a bright golden brown that caught the light and gleamed.

Vana gasped. The Finishers—or Finisher, if this was one of them coming to talk to her—apparently didn't bother with clothes. And apparently this Finisher, or all of them, or whatever, had poked around Vana's head looking for something she'd like.

She tried not to stare at the pert, small breasts that looked like they begged to be touched, or the nipples, slightly too big for them, or the long legs that went on forever. The legs were a bit out of proportion, but Vana couldn't bring herself to care.

"Um," Vana began, but she couldn't think of what to say or how to say it, and the finger behind the Finisher was growing extra eyes. They darted around, glancing at Vana like they knew they'd made some mistake but not what it was. "It's nothing, don't worry." Better a sexy girl than a giant squid or something.

"We are the Finishers. We wander the empty places until we are called."

"The empty places. Space?"

"Space?"

"Like where I found you. Not on any planets. Or near any suns."

"Space. We rest in… space. Until we are called."

"Okay, so you know what I mean by space, then. But I don't know what you mean. You hang around in space?"

A wry grin. Clearly a wry grin. "We are patient."

No, you're not.

Vana tried not to smirk right back. Whatever the Finishers were, they were powerful. And compared to them, Vana was tiny. Probably annoying. Like a bug that had flown too close to them and now they had to deal with it.

But apparently even godlike entities that floated around in deep space got bored sometimes, and that made Vana feel better.

Still, it would probably be rude to mention it. "So you wait around in space, floating there, with all different faces and limbs—"

"We are multitudes. Our memory spans eons."

Okay, now I know you're bored.

"Sure. You float around talking to each other—"

Thinking.

If anything, the voice was even sultrier inside Vana's head. The one voice was still the loudest, but all the others wove through Vana's head, teasing. All they needed to do was think, and they could be anywhere inside her head.

Could make her knees weak. But she shouldn't think about that. Not when it was so easy for them to go exploring in her head.

"Thinking, then. Not talking." Vana waved her arms vaguely. "Communicating. With each other. Until you're called."

"Yes."

Vana wasn't sure whether to be relieved or disappointed that they'd said it out loud.

"So what happens when you're called, then?"

The Finisher—no, *Finishers*, since making a human-shaped thing out of themselves didn't make them separate individuals—reached out a hand to touch Vana's arm. Their fingertips were warm, warmer than a human's, and Vana's skin tingled under them.

And not just because the girl-form was hot. She felt little pinpricks, like actual electricity. "What are you?" Vana whispered again.

What would beings like this be called to do? What would it be like to hang around on your home planet, going about your business, having a normal, boring day, and then see *that* descend from the sky?

The Finishers hadn't threatened her. But Vana felt the panic peek out from its hiding place in her head again. Her breath sped up and her head started to spin.

The Finishers stepped closer, half soothing warmth, half ozone crackle. Their mouth opened and closed, inhaling and exhaling, slow and steady. Vana shook her head. This was weird. It felt good, talking to a commune of aliens in the form of a sexy girl and laughing because they got bored.

But whatever the Finishers were, they weren't just friendly. And doing breathing exercises with them wouldn't make things better.

They ignored her. Or pretended to ignore her, anyway. Vana was pretty sure the muscle underneath her was sprouting eyes and ears. But the avatar in front of her only breathed, over and over, again and again. Inhale. Exhale. Inhale. Exhale.

Inhale. Exhale. Vana found herself doing it too. Why fight the rhythm when the Finishers were trying to keep her calm?

Their face was close to hers now. Little pinpricks of lightning arced from their lips to Vana's, and Vana wondered if they'd kiss her, and kind of hoped they would.

"Called," she said instead. "What do you mean when you say you're called?"

Light swirled in the Finishers' eyes, a flicker of angry gold.

"You don't want me to ask you, do you?"

"You don't want us to answer, human Vana."

Vana felt brave. Now that she could breathe again. "Look, Finishers. I already know you're dangerous. You tore my ship to scrap, and the only reason I'm breathing at all is because you're helping. You could easily kill me if you wanted to."

"We end worlds, Vana."

"You end worlds." Vana didn't know what she'd expected, but she knew that wasn't it. "Entire worlds?"

"We are the Finishers. We are called to worlds. We sense the life within them, and we do what we must do."

Vana's throat felt dry again. "You kill everyone."

"We walk among the living, and they end."

Vana shivered. "Why?"

"All worlds must end."

Vana looked at the woman in front of her, the almost but not quite perfect proportions, the eyes too bright to belong to a real human. She felt the lightning prick her skin. She stumbled back, not wanting to feel it again.

If this girl, this gorgeous girl, with her breath that saved Vana and her arms that crumpled metal and her fingers that melted it down, went walking through a trade outpost on an asteroid somewhere in the Third Frontier, what would happen?

Would she grow an eye or a mouth or a tentacle, like some character from a movie, and kill everyone in the market? Just because she—just because they—could?

She could imagine it easily, and that made things worse. Their lightning, streaking up to the clouds and down from the sky, sending jolts through everything on the ground—

Vana's heart raced. But it only made her angry. *No. I made it this far. I'm not gonna panic again.*

Especially not if that means the Finishers save me again.

She fought the dizziness and forced herself upright. Forced herself to breathe, without help from the Finishers. Forced words out of her tightening throat. "You didn't kill me."

"It is not your time." The Finishers pulled at her mind again. Memories flickered through her head: a childhood friend threatened by Legion thugs, a raid with the other Defiers, the sight of one of the motherships hit by a Legion torpedo and bursting into flame.

Whatever they were looking for, it wasn't something fun.

"Don't," Vana started to say.

Their voice was light, laughing and musical. "From your memories of war, it seems your own species wants to do our work for us."

Vana winced. Was that the Finishers' version of a joke? The fight against the Legion, the fight that had stranded Vana out here in the middle of nowhere? The fight that had killed more than one of Vana's friends? "What the hell is wrong with you?"

The Finishers blinked. "Wrong with us? For saying it is not your time? It would be better, then, for us to come?"

"No!" Vana ran at the avatar and shoved as hard as she could, heedless of the electricity, the warmth. Of the way its skin gave when she pressed against it, like the blow meant nothing, and the way they reformed again. "No! I don't want you coming anywhere near us!"

"We will not. We have no reason. Your world is young and strong and can bear bleeding."

"And that's supposed to reassure me?"

The avatar frowned. "We do not know."

Vana scowled and took a cautious step toward the avatar. *We don't know* wasn't very reassuring, but at least it was honest. At least they weren't trying to pretend they knew how to make Vana feel better.

But apparently they did want to make sure Vana didn't panic again. They were doing the breathing thing, with closed eyes and outstretched hands. They even grew a few mouths in their palms and hummed a little song, slow and steady and lulling.

"You smashed up my ship, but you kept me alive. And you breathed with me when I was having a panic attack. You're still breathing like that now."

They opened their eyes again. "That is so." Their mouth curled up in grin, coy and subtle. But Vana looked down at the mouth beside her, and that one was grinning, all angles and teeth and smugness.

You've got me, and you know it. But I've got something on you, too. "And you did that because you're bored?"

"We are multitudes. Our memory spans eons."

"You're also not very convincing. You said that already."

"It is the truth."

"It is," Vana said, trying to mimic the Finishers' tone, "the only thing you've been evasive about."

Their eyes widened, and Vana saw another flash of anger.

She stumbled back, only to remember she was standing in the middle of the Finishers' palm anyway. There was nowhere for her to go.

"We have our memories. And our connection." The principal voice was beautiful as always, and Vana wanted to drown in it. But the rest of the Finishers' voices were off, discordant, missing their harmony.

"But it's not enough, is it?"

"No."

"Is that why you found me?"

"You found us."

"So accidents do happen, then. Fair enough. Let me ask another question." Vana swallowed hard and stepped closer. "Is that why you poked around in my head? Is that why you took the form you did? Because you knew how much it would, uh, distract me?"

The avatar grinned. The bolder, bigger mouth on the floor stuck out its tongue and licked its lips.

"Wait. Hang on a second. I said you're hot, not that I actually go for giant aliens who are going to murder humanity someday."

The avatar stepped closer to Vana, hips swaying. Vana could have sworn their nipples hardened as she watched. Maybe too much, but Vana didn't mind. Couldn't mind, not with the Finishers' voices whispering seduction in a thousand tones Vana had never heard before and an almost human voice purring at her over them.

"You are interested," the Finishers whispered. "We have seen it."

"Okay. Fine. I am. But why are you, and more to the point, what the hell are you going to do with me once you're done?"

"Why," they repeated. It wasn't a question. "We end worlds. We come when we are called. We walk amid life. It chitters. It calls. It cries out. It moans. It," they hesitated, searching Vana's mind for a word, "dances. It... sings."

"And then you show up."

"We come when we are called. And the songs become screams, and the cries become wailing."

Vana winced. But the Finishers weren't done.

"Then all becomes silence."

Vana shuddered but didn't step back again. "And you don't like it."

They smiled, lopsided and toothy. It looked wrong on their beautiful face. "Visiting is... not unpleasant. But the silence afterward..." The multitude of voices trailed off, an uneasy hum.

"You don't like killing?"

"The silence afterward is eternal."

"That's why you're bored."

"We are multitudes. Our memory spans eons."

"Yeah, but you're by yourselves. You know each other already."

"We know ourselves. We are connected. We are one."

"But you're alone."

The Finishers looked down. Vana felt a sudden urge to brush the curly hair away from their face and—

What the hell. It's not like I'm going home anytime soon anyway. Vana reached out a hand and touched their hair. It felt soft like human hair, soft and fine. But the current ran through it like it ran through every part of the Finishers, and it sparked against Vana's fingers. She could see it, bright little sparks arcing toward her fingertips and grounding themselves there.

The Finishers' hair was alive, like any other part of them. It wasn't dead protein, growing out of follicles. It was living stuff, shaped and crafted and made small.

How many minds did the Finishers have? How many beings was Vana touching right now? How many of them were feeling her touch, like she'd wanted them to almost from the beginning, without her even realizing it.

Before she could think twice about it, Vana wrapped her hand around the back of the Finishers' head and drew their lips to hers.

They knew what to do. Were they reading Vana's mind again, or did it come with taking a new form? They opened their mouth and deepened the kiss. A hand pressed against Vana's back and pulled her closer.

The lips under Vana's mouth vibrated, full of warm, busy energy. Were they shifting again?

Vana clutched them tight. *I like you better like this.*

The skin of their back rippled under Vana's hands. Vana felt rough, leathery hide, a latticework of scales, soft fur her fingers sank into. Even a tiny mouth that opened at her touch and nipped, playful, at her fingertips.

Their human voice moaned. The echoes trilled and chittered and hummed. They sounded almost surprised, somewhere under their delight. *So this is what a kiss feels like.*

Vana was the one who'd showed them. She was touching a whole world's worth of beings, and they liked it. She sank into the feeling.

The Finishers reached for her. Fingers pressed against her skin, trickled like water, and solidified again, wound around her back.

"Wait," she gasped, breaking the kiss. The Finishers' lips quivered as she pulled away, and Vana heard a birdlike keen of dismay. "I'm not leaving, I just—I don't change shape like you. And it's probably me you want to touch, not just my clothes."

She blinked, shocked by her own words. Sure, she'd decided to go with this; it had worked out so far. She'd gone this fast before with human women, throwing herself into every touch and kiss before her nerves could catch up with her. And she usually didn't regret it. Out on the Third Frontier, you did what you wanted and did it as fast as you could, so the Legion couldn't show up to catch you.

But the Finishers were aliens, and just because they were bored didn't make this a good idea.

It's a terrible idea. They wrecked my ship. But what else am I gonna do? And when else am I gonna get the chance to show a whole tribe of aliens what sex is?

But before Vana could twist herself out of the Finishers' embrace and peel her shirt off, she felt them root around in her mind again. They were asking a question, it seemed. They wanted to find out—

—what clothes were. Thin fingers slipped under Vana's shirt and pulled it over her head with dexterity Vana would've sworn they'd practiced if she didn't know better. Then the slim fingers unclasped her bra. Vana watched it slip through the floor made of the Finishers' palm, to land gods only knew where. The floor of the ship, maybe, wherever that was. If it still existed.

Vana chewed her lip. She'd decided not to care. She focused on the Finishers in front of her, their shape still mostly human, and grinned. Their eyes widened, the lids pulling back a little too far. Tiny extra eyes appeared under the first pair and blinked at Vana.

"Like what you see?" she teased.

They pressed a hand to her chest, above her heart. Their touch was warm and curious, and Vana guessed it was feeling her heartbeat. That was cute, too innocent for a deathbringing monster, and Vana laughed and shook her chest in another invitation.

But Vana wasn't the only one who could be touched. She copied their gesture, wanting to feel their skin changing shape under her hands again. She cupped her hand around their breast, feeling the first quivering of movement as the texture rippled again.

"You like this," Vana whispered. "You're so excited you can't hold yourselves together."

The Finishers swiped out with their other hand. Vana felt something sharp and froze, her chest constricting. She knew they didn't mean to hurt her, but if they made a mistake, the gods only knew what they might do.

She let out her breath, slow and easy. *I'm fine. I'm fine.* The Finishers' claws hadn't cut her, just left pink little lines in her skin. They stung, but no worse than any human lover's fingernails might.

But they had ripped through her pants and torn through her underwear. Fabric fell away from her in sad tatters before a fleshy wave swallowed it up.

Vana felt a little tingle and tensed, but it wasn't panic making her heart race. Not when the Finishers' mock-breath was still there, under it all, ready to catch her if she fell into her fear. *All right then. I see how it is.*

The clawed hand lingered, pressed against Vana's bare stomach, halfway between a raptor's taloned foot and a woman's fingertips. Vana held her breath and waited, and another appendage, feathered like a wing, moved soft and silken down her belly.

Vana raised an eyebrow and grabbed at whatever passed for the Finishers' wrist. "Not so fast. I'm supposed to be showing you what to do." Feathers fluttered under her hand, a sudden burst of protest, and then stilled.

Vana let go of the feathery claw or hand or wingtip and pressed her hand to the Finishers' hip. Something moved against her palm, silken-soft and scurrying.

"Settle down," Vana said. She'd spent so long being frightened, fleeing the Legion's horrors and the ones in her own mind. Now someone else felt nervous instead. Someone powerful and strange and ancient. Thousands of minds, all wanting her touch to soothe them.

I could get used to this.

The skin under Vana's hand puckered, a clinging little suction cup, and then it smoothed out again.

"That's better." Vana hoped she sounded sultry and commanding. The Finishers stopped moving, and the energy crackled all around her, and they didn't need to plead for Vana to know what they wanted.

She slid her fingers downward. The Finishers' skin surged with warmth. Energy crackled over it, and Vana thought she felt something that could have been motion, but it didn't matter, not when she could tell the Finishers were trying as hard as they could to be still.

The Finishers tugged at her mind again, sharp and

electric and urgent. Vana suspected they were rifling through her brain to find out about sex. They'd mimicked a human body well enough for Vana to like it. But now they needed to know what a human body did when someone touched it.

And they'd apparently figured it out, because when Vana slipped two fingers down to touch the Finishers' labia, they were silken-soft and slick with wetness. Vana gasped and felt her own sex pulse in answer.

The Finishers made a small sound, echoing Vana's gasp too well, like a talking bird mimicking its owner.

"All right," Vana said, sliding her fingers over the slick skin. "But you're not me. If I wanted myself, I'd touch myself instead of you. So show me how you feel."

The Finishers tipped their head back, opened their mouth, and cried out in a cacophony of sound. A bird's coo, a primate's shriek, an insect's eager clicking, a tinkling sound like breaking glass. The thrum of something else Vana couldn't place, and a sound she had no name for that vibrated all through the Finishers' body and made the skin pressed to Vana's fingers quiver.

They'd forgotten their human voice, apparently. Buried it under the thousands of others they'd borrowed. Vana thought she could hear it, somewhere in the whirlwind, but maybe she wanted to because she liked it best.

The morass of sound wasn't pretty. It stung Vana's ears, jarring and loud. If Vana hadn't ordered the Finishers to make it, the sound would've sent Vana spiraling. It reminded her the Finishers were nothing like her, not really. Not under the skin they'd copied from some scraps of fantasy and memory in their new pet human's mind.

But they were making it for Vana. Because she'd told them to.

"You really haven't felt anything like this before, have you?" Vana whispered, in awe.

She felt their answer in her mind, a burst of activity blipping through her neurons.

"I didn't think so," Vana said. "Can you lie down? It's

easier to reach you that way."

The Finishers curled around themselves, bending their knees in ways a human didn't bend. They meant to obey, to give Vana access, but instead it made her yelp. They weren't hurting themselves, but seeing a human twist into that shape made Vana think of pain.

Their eyes widened, and their brow furrowed in a very human expression of worry. They unbent their knees with a weird little pop and Vana sighed in relief. The skin of the massive palm they were standing on shifted into a ledge, festooned with eyes, mouths, and fingertips. The avatar tilted back to meet it and lay there, a woman's shape laid out on a living bed that whispered its eagerness.

That was still weird, but at least it didn't look painful. And they wanted her, and she was already used to that. She stepped closer and leaned down over their avatar.

She let herself drink the sight in: light brown skin, a little too orange, golden to match the gold-flecked eyes, which blinked back at Vana with a slow, steady rhythm. High cheekbones and a thin nose, but thick, ample lips. Vana almost laughed. They were beautiful like this, but a little mismatched. Like they'd plucked all kinds of different features from Vana's head, hoping the combination would excite her more than anything else. Their breasts were the same, small and tight with thick nipples and wide brown areolas.

Exaggerations, again, Vana guessed, but her cunt spasmed again in expectation. The avatar they'd made looked like a single human body—but it was plural, plural and present and waiting, built up out of a hundred women Vana had touched or kissed or wanted, waiting for her.

She pressed her hand to their stomach again, the slight roundness to their belly. It was soft and warm, and tingling with that inhuman energy. The flesh under her fingers quivered, and she felt the power beneath. But the Finishers didn't change shape, not visibly.

"Good," she said. It was absurd that they obeyed. Absurd that they obeyed Vana, who got in the other Defiers' way, with her shortness of breath and her panic and her getting lost. Absurd that they obeyed a human at all. Absurd that they stared at her like her approval mattered.

Unable to shapeshift, they settled for canting their hips and making a small noise, like a cat's mewl with little bells ringing behind it. Something reached out from the makeshift bed and clutched at her leg

"I said don't." Vana glared down at the offending appendage. "I'm touching you now."

It retreated, hastily obedient. Vana chuckled and moved her hands between their legs again. She sought out their clit with her fingers, rubbing in a slow, teasing rhythm. They closed their eyes, and other eyes blinked open in their skin, watching Vana with eager curiosity.

Skin smoothed over the panoply of eyes again. The Finishers pressed their flesh against her hand, insistent, and the electric heat stung the tips of her fingers. That drove her on, her cunt pulsing in sympathy at her partners' eagerness. She moved her fingers faster, rougher, not bothering with subtlety.

The Finishers cried out again, the human-sounding moan fading into a bird's trill, a low groan vibrating under it. They moved their hips again, grinding against Vana's fingers. Something reached out for Vana again, soft against the skin of her legs. Something smooth and warm, like water, trickled down one of Vana's thighs.

Vana had to fight not to spread her own legs, to not let the Finishers touch her, to not find out all the ways that they could caress and claim her. "Not yet," she said, her own voice breathy and hoarse in her ears.

The trickling water pulled away again, and Vana pressed her legs together for a moment, missing its warmth. But the Finishers wanted to know what it felt like to be touched, and Vana wouldn't dream of distracting them.

She moved her fingers on their clit again, slow this time and firm, and parted their labia with her other hand. They gasped, something between a spoken word and a sharp intake of breath. Vana let out a laugh. *You're not the one who breathes, after all.*

She slipped two fingers down to their entrance and paused there. Little bursts of energy zipped over her fingertips.

"Yes," the Finishers sang, only one of their voices human.

Vana slid her fingers in, slow as she could stand. The strange flesh the Finishers had crafted was soft inside, soft and warm as anyone she'd touched, and it shifted to admit her, opening and opening.

She figured she could let that disobedience go. She pushed in slow and easy, and the Finishers moved against her hand again, wanting more. She flicked her thumb against their clit, and they buzzed in pleased surprise.

"More," the Finishers begged, an avalanche of voices.

Vana obliged, quickening her pace, moving fast and hard as they rocked to meet her. Something inside them changed, and she felt their walls brush against her fingers, an eerie caress.

Strange enough to make her pause and let them grip her, moving muscles no human had. She had the dim sense that some other humans—whoever they were, wherever they were— would find it weird, maybe even creepy.

Their loss.

She brought another finger to their entrance. They spread their legs, in some weird way that defied the laws of physics. Vana didn't bother to figure it out. She slid her third finger inside. Their walls spasmed, tightening around her again, and rippled against her fingers.

Vana moved and they keened, and Vana laughed at them. She didn't know what the Finishers would make of themselves, what their cunt would become, what they might do to tease her thrusting fingers.

But she knew she wanted to touch every part of them she could. She pushed deep, not bothering to move her thumb against their clit again. *I want you to feel this. I want you to remember me inside you.*

She thought they were going to move with her again, but

instead their whole body moved. The flesh roiled in a tremulous wave, and the avatar's edges shimmered. Shadows of legs and arms flickered near its shoulders and hips.

That's what else you could have been, isn't it? What else you'll become if you lose control. Vana laughed, a full-throated chuckle. She pulled her fingers free almost all the way and grinned in satisfaction when the Finishers shivered and dissolved again.

"Please." It wasn't a word, just part of one, an atom of speech that became wailing beasts, tinkling glass, a whine of need and a snatch of song.

Vana rammed her fingers in, all subtlety forgotten. She thrust once, twice, three times, then plunged deep, running her thumb over their clit again.

Their cunt spasmed around her fingers, and they let go completely.

Everything around Vana changed. Heat and light thrilled all around her, and the Finishers' flesh melted and doubled. A thousand eyes stared at Vana, then rolled back in their sockets. Some became mouths, open and singing. Bells pealed and birds cawed, and somewhere a great beast roared its pleasure. Thin insect legs grabbed at Vana's hips and softened. She passed into them, like stepping into a mirror.

Everything was light and heat, light and heat and the breath that had saved her and soothed her, bubbling up to carry her away with it. She moved her own legs apart and something filled her, shapeless at first, then a shadow of the fingers she'd used herself, then something else entirely. Something lapped at her cunt—apparently they'd learned something about that from rooting around in her mind.

But they weren't trying to fuck her, not really. They were letting her feel what they felt, the strange pleasure overtaking them, something they'd never given into before. She closed her eyes and moved her hand again, not sure what she was touching any more.

Heat and light enveloped her and filled her. It burst forth from her mouth, her cunt. It spasmed all around her, a tight embrace that didn't hurt, that never could. It tensed around her fingers and shivered in her belly.

Overcome, she closed her eyes.

Vana was floating. Floating and naked. She didn't know where, but the little thrills of aftershock trilling through her flesh meant she'd just had sex. Really good sex. She pressed her legs together and waited a long moment before finally opening her eyes.

Something blinked at her. A massive cat's eye, speckled yellow and green, winking open—from the wall? She rubbed her eyes and blinked. What was it you were supposed to do to make sure you weren't dreaming? Pinch yourself?

"Human," said a voice. A beautiful voice, with other voices threaded under it. And a few weird sounds.

Oh. Right.

Vana took a few deep breaths, just to reassure herself she still could, and then spoke. "Finishers. Hey."

"Our memory—"

Vana waved a hand to cut them off. "You said that before. More than once. You have a perfect memory. I know."

"We share this," they answered. "We remember this."

The wall parted, a fleshy clinging, and the avatar emerged out of it, smiling broadly. Maybe too wide, but Vana didn't mind so much. When the face they chose had lips like that, they could get things a little wrong.

Vana chuckled. "So what is this, you're thanking me?"

The Finishers stepped closer. They reached out to trace a long finger over Vana's cheek. Static crackled where they touched her. "Yes," their chorus of voices said. "We thank you."

Vana wrapped her hand around theirs and held it against her chin. It felt human and alien all at once. "You're welcome."

They didn't answer. Just blinked at Vana, slow and calm, like a contented cat.

Vana wanted to touch their hair. To pull them in close for a kiss. To do anything and everything she wanted because this was as weird as a dream. And as good.

But their words came unbidden to her mind, piercing her calm.

We end worlds, Vana.

We walk among the living and they end.

What would happen to her world if the Finishers got too close?

She sighed, savoring the feeling of her lovers' strange flesh. Then, with another deep breath, she forced herself to pull away.

The Finishers blinked at her again. It wasn't smooth and easy this time. "We do not understand."

"What happens now?"

The Finishers reached for her again, their fingers growing long and spindly, the nails becoming pointed claws. "We do not understand."

Well, at least that made this easier. Vana put her hands on her hips, trying to summon up the commanding voice she'd used before. "You broke my ship. You picked me up out of the wreckage. You made sure that I could breathe."

"We did." Their smile curled, lopsided, like it might melt off their face if they didn't concentrate. Vana curled her hands into fists at her sides and pressed her nails into her palms.

"You had fun with me. Learned what it felt like to be touched."

"We greatly enjoyed what you offered us. Yes." The clawed fingers smoothed, glimmering with something that looked like oil.

Vana didn't step any closer. She let out a slow breath and tried to ignore the way her throat tensed up when she inhaled again. "Now you've got what you wanted, so what are you going to do with me?"

"What do you wish?"

"We're out in the middle of nowhere. I mean, it doesn't bother you. You don't even need to breathe. But I'm stranded."

They rummaged through her mind, a gentle pull. Too

gentle. *Don't make this harder than it already is. Don't make me miss you.*

"Do you want us to return you to"—shuffle, shuffle—"the Third Frontier? You were misplaced."

"I got lost, yeah. But you wrecked my ship, and the mothership that deployed it is long gone by now. The Defiers don't stay in one place." *Not if we want to stay alive, anyway.*

"A planet, then." They hummed, pleased with themselves. "One of the colony worlds."

Colony worlds, colony worlds, colony worlds. The echo was a morass of sound, but all Vana could hear were those words, over and over. They played over and over in her mind, until her head started to pound and her heart rate sped up.

Damn it. Not now.

The Finishers tilted their head, like a confused puppy.

We walk among the living, and they end.

"I don't think you can take me home."

Their neck curled too far and their eyes grew wide, opening and opening.

"You can't follow me!"

"Can't? We may do as we wish."

Vana's throat tightened. "You end worlds."

"Yes."

"Then what happens when you follow me to mine?"

The Finishers' head snapped up. They blinked at Vana with eyes that took up half their face. "We end worlds when we are called, yes."

"And what happens when you're not?"

"We do not know."

Vana's mouth fell open. The Finishers had the sense to stop with their wide-eyed cute animal imitation and shrink their eyes again. They opened their mouth like they wanted to ask a question, but they must not have found the words. All that came out was a high-pitched, quizzical buzz.

"You don't know," Vana echoed, her voice flat. The familiar, anxious tension in her chest didn't even bother her. It felt vaguely like a friend. *Appropriate emotional reaction, check.*

"You offer to take me back to my base, but when I ask you what will happen when you do, you tell me you don't know?"

"We have never done this before." There was something strange behind their words. Something off. Usually, when they spoke the other voices sounded like echoes. Sounded like they agreed, somehow, even if all they were doing was growling or purring or chirping or moaning.

This sounded different. Off, like a band that wasn't playing in tune.

You're arguing, aren't you?

Vana felt a pinprick of emotion. Annoyance, aggravation, something. Was that how she felt, underneath panic that looked vaguely like calm? Or was she picking it up from them? "No, you've never done this before. That's why you tried it."

"That is so. But we," their voices dissolved into a morass of noise, then coalesced into something Vana could understand, "will protect you. We did so before. We... are doing so now. You... need our help to..."

"Breathe."

"Yes. If we could not preserve life, you would not be... breathing... now."

"But you said you don't know what will happen if you come back with me."

A whirlwind of sound. Their skin shimmered and vibrated. They grew new limbs and pointed them at themselves, accusing. Something like a hammer pounded, over and over. Vana put a hand to her head. If they kept this up, even their calm breathing thing wouldn't pull her out again.

Not soon enough to make sure they didn't do something stupid, anyway.

She drew in as deep a breath as her panicking body would allow and screamed. "Shut up!"

Total silence followed, not a skitter or a hum. Vana didn't like it. Was this how being alone had sounded before everything turned into something from some crazy dream?

A light pulsed, rhythmic and slow. *Remember to breathe. Remember to breathe.*

Vana did. "Listen. You're protecting me right now. I'm glad. I might be dead by now if you weren't. I don't know if you're messing with spacetime, and even if you're not, I don't even know how much life support I had left."

A staticky, distant, robotic chime. Apparently her ship's computer was still trying to answer. She smiled weakly and went on talking. "I appreciate you protecting me. I enjoyed the hell out of you having sex with me. But just because you protected me doesn't mean it's safe to take me home. Not if you don't know what will happen when we get there."

"We will protect you," they said again.

"All protecting me proves is you don't always kill everyone."

"You matter to us. The others do not."

Well, there it was. "And you don't care what happens to them. Because you happened to meet me."

"We have no reason to care for them." They thumbed through Vana's mind again. "And there is a war among them anyway."

"That's none of your business."

"It brought you to us."

"So you're gonna keep me and murder everyone else? Everything else?"

"You do not wish it."

"No, I don't wish it! Of course I don't wish it! It's wrong."

"Ending worlds is our purpose."

"So you think I want you to end mine?"

"Our purpose is not wrong."

Vana gaped at them. What could she—what could any human—even say to that?

She stared at the body they'd picked for themselves. Of course it was gorgeous. Of course it was perfect. They'd plucked it right out of Vana's own head. But it wasn't them, not really.

She'd let herself believe it was. Let them trick her into thinking it. Let herself think the avatar was who they really were. A curious, sexy human, with a few weird echoes in her voice and a few extra limbs when she got too excited.

But the avatar wasn't them. The weird limbs were them. The floor made from a hand was them. The wide-open mouths and weird clusters of eyes were them.

The bubble of air letting Vana breathe was them.

"Look, I don't... You've been good to me. And I only know the world I've got. But I'm not like you. I'm not a whole planetful of consciousnesses all jammed together. I'm a human. One random, single, solitary human."

"You require others."

"Yes, I require others! Don't you? You've had yourselves to keep you company for millions of years, or something—"

"Since what you know as time began."

"Fine. My point is, you got bored, and there's millions of you."

"We number beyond counting. We are the Finishers."

"Lots of you, and only one of me. And even you couldn't handle being all alone. What makes you think I can?"

"You matter to us. Your enemies do not."

Vana tightened her hands into fists. Not that a human fist would do anything against them. They'd probably catch it, like some slime creature from one of the Inner Worlds or something. But she had to do something. Spit in the Finishers' eyes, even if she had liked them and they'd—

Liked her.

Wait.

"Enemies. You just said 'your enemies.' As in 'Your enemies don't matter.' Not 'the others,' like you said before."

"That is so."

"Wait, you're... you're offering to end the war?"

"If we can, yes."

"You can do that? Come for the Legion and leave the rest of us alone?"

Her heart raced. She shouldn't even think it. The Legion were nasty bastards, yes. Even people too scared or too peaceful to join the Defiers flew off to the Frontiers to get away from them. And the Defiers didn't always fight fair. They couldn't, not against an enemy that owned most of the quadrant.

But Vana had seen the Finishers' power firsthand. Hell, she was only alive right now because they'd made bits of themselves into a terrarium.

Using power like that wasn't winning a war. It was blinking and making your enemy disappear. Vana blinked. *Why am I the one who has to figure this out?*

She wasn't a squad captain, or a general, or a leader. She wasn't one of the thinkers who decided on tactics or the writers whose pamphlets spread the word about Defiance. She was one random person, one of thousands who'd flown off to the Frontiers and joined the Defiers because they had to do something.

And yet.

The Defiers risked their lives with every raid. Vana had risked hers, over and over.

If you got lost... well. If the Finishers hadn't found Vana, she would've been as good as dead anyway. That wouldn't have been fancy and honorable. That would have been starving to death in the middle of nowhere or opening an airlock to go quicker.

None of them would have to do it again. Not if the Finishers were right about this. Vana let out a slow breath. This got more and more like a dream the more she was in it. *Oh, here, it's the ultimate weapon. It just happened to be lying around out in space somewhere. Oh, and it likes getting fucked.*

"You're sure about this? You're not going to show up and everybody dies because you made a mistake?"

"We are not certain, no. But we were not called. And when we are not called, we may do as we wish." Their mouth yawned open and became a forest of teeth, rows upon rows of little sharp ones. "You have given us a gift, Vana."

"So... What? So this is paying me back for the sex we had?"

"We are grateful. We are pleased." Thrum, hum, buzz. All in a rough sort of harmony. They meant it. "We will end your enemies for you, if you wish it."

The end of the war. As a present. How many of the Defiers would say yes before the Finishers were even done talking?

But when Vana had joined the Defiers, vaporizing her enemies wasn't quite what she'd had in mind. Driving them off was. Getting them to leave the Frontiers alone was.

Even overthrowing them was a pipe dream. At least to Vana. Maybe not to the men and women who wrote the manifestoes and gave the speeches. But Vana... Vana was angry. Vana wanted to be free.

What the hell did she say? What the hell could she say?

"I don't know."

It was the only thing that didn't make her heart freeze in her chest. That and, "You can't just send me home?"

Teeth upon teeth upon teeth. "You said it yourself, human. We have found that we dislike being alone."

"Was that a threat?" Vana took a step back, but kept staring straight at them, hoping she'd come off powerful and strong, like she had before, when the Finishers were following her orders.

They buzzed and yowled. Some of them wailed. Vana held her ground. Were they yelling at her or at themselves?

The monstrous face shrank, the toothed mouth pursing into human lips, the eyes becoming small and almond. Curly hair grew out around it, and the Finishers looked back at her with their human face. "We are grateful. We are pleased. We will not do you harm, Vana. We will... we will not do harm to any human, if you bid us leave them be. We must come if we are called, but otherwise..."

"You'll leave, if I tell you to?"

"Correct. We will reunite you with your mothership. And then we will leave, if that is what you wish."

They looked down, their hair falling in front of their face. But Vana could see enough of it to catch their expression. A childish pout, so exaggerated it would've been funny if Vana didn't know they weren't human. An eye sprouted out from their bellybutton and blinked at her, slow and mournful.

"What about not killing anyone and not leaving either?"

The eye became a mouth. It smiled. The Finishers looked up again and raised a hand to brush their hair out of their face.

The mouth on their face was smiling too. Energy crackled in the gap between their lips. "Not leaving? The humans would notice us. We are as large as a planet."

Now it was Vana's turn to smile. "Do you have to be?"

The shape that the Finishers had taken was strange. Compressed and cramped, the energy that connected them all zipping through tiny channels, their best guess at what Vana called veins. Wearing a human's skin was easier when they didn't have to remember not to grow extra legs, or spare hands. Or more than two eyes. How did humans look at anything?

They couldn't. Not really. They shook the one head they'd permitted themselves and followed Vana, who walked ahead of them.

Her walk was... pleasant to observe. It would never change shape, but they weren't sure they minded. They felt something like heat stir in the places Vana had touched before and smiled at her back. Perhaps this form had some advantages.

They felt fragile. Perhaps even breakable. These small, short-lived creatures could never harm them, of course—they could simply shift in response—but they could almost imagine what it might be like to be afraid.

They'd taken small forms before. Sometimes when they were called, they'd grown so large they blocked out the sun of whatever world they meant to end. Sometimes they savored the fear of beings who knew they were coming and knew they could do nothing. And sometimes they took the smallest and most insignificant form they could find on a world they visited, and only made themselves known as death and devastation spread.

But it was strange to be small now. To be restricted.

Caught in this form, unable to change it as their wills dictated. Because if they did, these humans would know they were not what they seemed.

It was stranger still when the other humans came to crowd around them. They could smell their curiosity, could taste their confusion.

"This woman helped you get back?" one of them asked.

Vana laughed. "They. Not she." The laughter of only one voice was thin, thin and soft, but it warmed them again. Vana had given them a gift, and they were grateful. "They saved my life. I have no doubt I would've died out there without them."

They smiled. It seemed appropriate. They resisted the urge to grow a few more mouths.

The human, a male, narrowed his eyes at her and shook his head at Vana. Probably disbelief, but they didn't dare go into his mind to find out. Not until they knew how a human—other than Vana—might react to that sort of thing.

That was strange too, to keep themselves in check. They'd done it for pleasure before. For the novelty.

They were not sure they liked it now.

The other human was laughing. "So you get separated from the mothership, wander around the void for a few days, and come back with a girlfriend none of us have met?"

The Finishers held out their hand. They wanted to grow a mouth filled with narrow, pointed teeth, but refrained.

They needed something to do between cleansings, and if they made a mistake Vana would send them away. And they would obey, they knew, even the reluctant ones. They owed her that much.

They wanted much more.

"Hello," they said.

ABOUT THE AUTHOR

Alexa Black lives in the Washington, DC, area where she works as a peer mentor and advocate for people with disabilities. She has a master's degree in philosophy from Georgetown University, but has always returned to her passion for writing. Though a philosopher by training, she would rather inflict complicated questions on her characters than lecture about them. When not writing, she can be found gaming, seeking out new restaurants to try, or drinking too many lattes. She has published one novel with Supposed Crimes, *Salvation* (written under the pen name A. M. Hawke) and two with Bold Strokes Books, *Steel and Promise* (a Lambda Literary award finalist in the Erotica category) and *The Outcasts*. The stories in this collection have been published before in anthologies for Supposed Crimes or by Less Than Three Press.

www.ingramcontent.com/pod-product-compliance
Lightning Source LLC
Chambersburg PA
CBHW071835190726

48292CB00005B/1782